MURDER IN THE HIGHEST PLACES

Alfred John Dalrymple

Dart

Copyright 1998 by Alfred John Dalrymple
Second edition 2002
Third edition 2012
Fourth edition 2015...for Amazon "Createspace".

ISBN: 0967333814
ISBN 13: 9780967333816

This book may not be reproduced in whole or in part, by any means, without permission, except in cases of brief quotations in critical articles and reviews.

Published by Dart Books:
P.O. Box 744, Unalaska, AK 99685
907-581-3701
P.O. Box 149, Northwood, N.H. 03261
603-942-5993

CHAPTER ONE

In the car's passenger seat, sat a middle-age man, graying and heavy, but somewhat handsome in a business suit of dark brown. He said "Slow down among these houses. If you get stopped for speeding, the deal is off. Also, the roads are slippery. This is early March…and the bareness has ice in it. Do you know who I am, kid?"

The driver, a tall, blond man, tanned and youthful, said "I assume you have power in New Hampshire."

"I'll be governor in a year or two. Later, today, I'll pocket twenty million dollars." He raised his shoulders. "Land development. Not bragging, son, just telling you to be careful. So…you're about twenty five? Now…how would you describe yourself?"

"I'm a murderer!"

The passenger said "Pull into the shopping center. Go to where the cars are gathered."

They stopped very near a car, and the passenger looked through his own window, apparently to see if he had room to open the door. Then he gave the driver a white envelope, the size of typing paper.

"This is the man I want killed. The information is here, and the money. Don't read it now! Get to Concord, and onto a bus for Boston. The jet leaves for Nepal, by way of Bangkok...at six o'clock." He reached to the driver and tapped the envelope. "The man left yesterday...and I want you on his heels."

The driver opened the envelope. "The man's name is Oliver Faulkner?"

"Yes. A man you should kill quickly. You can go now!"

The driver removed the contents and put them on the seat. Picking up a photograph and a single sheet of paper, he said "Oliver Faulkner...age thirty five. He's three years older than I am."

"You're older than you look."

"A hundred and sixty pounds," continued the driver. If this is a recent picture, he doesn't weigh that...he's heavier. How tall is he?"

The passenger looked away, and leaned away, putting his hand on the door. Then he sat back and studied the other.

The driver said "If you want me on his heels, I need to see him."

"He's about six feet tall," said the passenger.

"It says "Five feet nine...also, handsome and intelligent."

The passenger said "I was planning to change those descriptions, and forgot to."

"I don't mean to contend, Mr. Wallace. Elmer...? Is this a picture of Mel Gibson...movie star?" He held the photo up and away. "Or is it Oliver Faulkner...a bit heavier and taller than you want him to be?"

2

Calmly, but with obvious irritation, the passenger said "I can call this off!"

"Mr. Wallace. I understand your anger. But I need the truth. You've got him at the top, with handsome and intelligent…and nearer to the bottom with thinner and shorter."

"Then I corrected it!"

"So you're afraid of what he knows…but, also, of what he is. Is that why you try to make him less than what he is?… in a dismissing, wishful way."

"I don't! And you better not!" snapped Wallace.

"What did he do?" asked the driver. I don't mean to pry, but…if you please, sir, I can do my job better."

"He slept with my wife!"

"Mr. Wallace, an hour ago I parked across from your house, and went to the saloon. I mentioned the name Oliver Faulkner, then sat awhile and listened. He didn't sleep with your wife. Sorry to be rude…but my job is quickly done, as you wish…if I know he's full of what sinks to the bottom, if given a nudge."

"He insulted my book!"

The driver reached inside his leather jacket, black and trim, to the inner chest pocket, and brought out a book of about fifty pages. Gently, he put it onto the seat, near the passenger's leg.

On the book sat a small, yellowed plastic bag. It had two locks of hair in it, one blond, the other brown.

"What's this?" asked Wallace, picking up the plastic bag.

The murderer snatched the plastic bag, and returned it to the inner pocket. He did this with a forced tightness at his mouth, and he looked away from Wallace. Then he returned to the book.

""In the Palm of the Lotus". Is this the work he insulted? Did your enemy say the thoughts herein are taken from others? But why would that bother you? You say, on the back cover, that you get to the highest places by reflecting greatness. So…he called you a mirror? No!…he called you a liar, who arranges words to say they're yours. Ah!…his insult is not why you hired me!"

The passenger shouted "You don't need to know why!"

"Mr. Wallace…you often visited the house of your neighbor and his thirteen year old daughter. Or, is it twelve? Sometimes the neighbor wouldn't be home. And Oliver Faulkner arrived, one day, and tossed you through the door. She's pregnant! Is that it?"

Mr. Wallace was red-faced.

"Not that I care," said the driver, in a softer tone. "I don't want your money…other than this." He held up the smaller white envelope. "It's because I need the truth. Oliver Faulkner can nail you down. Elmer Wallace…goodbye to moving up!"

Again Wallace shouted. "Listen…kid! You don't tell me anything about that girl…what she is or isn't. I can terminate this! You better shut up about what I did.

"Yes, sir!"

Wallace said "I know where up is! If you want the job, put that photo and money in your pocket. When you return I'll pay the other seventy five thousand."

The driver put these things into the inside pocket of his jacket, then he rested his hands on the steering wheel.

"My name is Curt. I'm told I had a mother and father until I was a year old. Then I was three years in an orphanage. I remember being alone and hungry and cold. When

I was four...someone gave me a little plastic bag and said it was my parent's hair in it. I..." He reached inside his jacket. I carried it here, in my shirt pocket."

Wallace yelled "Maybe you can't handle this job!"

"My parents came back!...for awhile...fighting. And then my father stopped pretending to care. He got mean to me."

"You're crazy!" Wallace was shaking his head. "Maybe I'll terminate this! But...can't you just forget it?"

The driver continued. "My father died when I was eight. He leaned through a window...way out...so I nudged him, firmly, and watched him bounce. Only my mother guessed it wasn't his choice. She left town, again...and I haven't seen her since. Which I'm happy to say!"

Wallace was staring. Softly, he said "What are you planning to do now, Curt? Will you go to Nepal?"

Curt said "You have power...and large plans. But you think of your self only."

"I give money to charity!" said Wallace. "Yes! And I can, because I'm the best at what I do. You'll be seeing me up there...in my place. So...is it goodbye, Curt? Are you off to Nepal?"

Curt said "I was a star athlete in high school...and managed the newspaper. I was the best waiter in New Haven, Connecticut. In the army I was the sharpest shooter, and dresser. Yes, I'm the best, too...Mr. Wallace. Now I'm going to Nepal, where I'll twist the nose of the enemy...the handsome and intelligent, Oliver Faulkner. The man on the top. You know what else I'll do?"

"No. What else?"

"I'll use his girlfriend. After he's dead I'll use his gear... to have a climb...above what you call the top."

Wallace waited a few seconds, then said "Bring me proof that he's dead!" He faced his own door, putting both hands against it. "And don't take forever!"

Curt reached into an outside pocket of his jacket and, withdrawing a knife, pressed a button on it, causing a narrow, three-sided blade to appear. So did a hand guard, to keep his hand from sliding along the knife.

He plunged it into the passenger's back. Four times. And at the last, he was able to hold it there awhile, having pinned the man's jacket collar against the door, to keep the scene intact...undisturbed by another's will.

CHAPTER TWO

Without counting, the young Nepali folded the rupees and slipped them into his pocket. "I would have come even if you didn't pay me."

"Thanks for walking with me, Sanu," said Oliver. He grasped his hand, then hugged him. "Take this trail, straight into Lukla. Ten minutes. I'll see you in Kathmandu, in a couple weeks. Dui hapta."

Sanu looked down. "You'll go to Tibet."

"I doubt it, Sanu."

"You won't come with me to my village." Now he looked into Oliver's eyes. "You said you would. My wife heard you say it. My son heard you."

Oliver said "So did I hear me. If I don't go to Tibet, I'll visit your village. You have my word."

Sanu pouted. "I dreamed that you fell in a high place."

"Did I survive it?"

"I don't know. MY wife kicked me at that moment."

"If I die up there...my soul will go with you to your village. I'll rap your head, like this." He reached out and rapped a knuckle on Sanu's head, twice. "So you'll know it's me."

Sanu smiled. "You feel good now? Strong? It takes three days, you said!"

"Yes, three days! And we walked five." He shifted the pack on his back, acknowledging the weight, and his comfort. "Namaste!"

"Namaste!" said Sanu, holding his hands together, above his head...and bowing.

———

They had walked five days in a moderate but long-houred manner. He had intended to spend the night in Lukla... for a hot shower...but soon figured he could get that in Namche, and have an extra day above. So...he watched his friend depart. Then he turned away.

It was a cool, sunny morning in early March, as he faced north.

Soon he would be well above Lukla and beginning to move around the mountain, northwestward. He would gradually descend until near the Dudh Kosi, the Milk River, and keep it almost constantly in view below, and to his left.

For an hour Oliver walked easily, usually among huge, mossy pine, and while looking down to the sunnied water. He was delighted, but doubted that he'd do it again.

He thought about the high-bridge river crossing, a couple hours ahead, where you can look far back along the river. Perhaps he'd stop there. If he thought about where he came from, maybe he'd know where he was going.

He said, aloud, "What a beautiful way to drift. And yet, this is where I ought to be. I feel it. I..." He scratched his head. "If you love being where you are, can you be lost?"

⇌

At Phakding he stopped for tea at a small hotel. It had two rooms, both upstairs...and, once before, he spent the night here. The building was yet in the trees, but near to the river, and there was a porch with two tables. He sat outside and had apple juice and fried rice with egg and chicken in it, and he had tea and chocolate cake.

The proprietor, a middle-age Nepali man, said "Hello. I've seen you here...other times." They shook hands. And the man asked "Where will you go?"

Oliver said "I don't know."

"You should be with someone," said the man. "Each time I've seen you...you've been alone." After Oliver said goodbye, and they shook hands, the man gave him a piece of cake wrapped in a napkin.

⇌

Before he got to the high bridge, Oliver passed through a place of huge boulders, jumbled together. The trail went between and under and on top of these, and he was interested in this. So, not attending closely to what was approaching, he suddenly was looking into the salve-red, puffy face of a woman…dull-eyed yet staring…being carried in the basket of a Nepali porter.

Oliver guessed that she came from above Pheriche, where others allowed her to stay after sickness showed and lingered. Now…he saw nothing in her eyes. He wondered if this shell would eat at the little hotel by the river. Then he was angry at himself for not thinking she could do that.

When he got to the high bridge, he was behind a heavily laden Nepali family of five. Two men led, bent under full baskets. An older woman, probably the grandmother, followed…then a girl about ten, and a boy six or seven. All carried the cone-shaped dhoka, and had goods for trading or selling at Nanche's bazaar.

They walked high above the swift water.

"Namaste!" said Oliver.

The whole family stopped and faced him, and said "Namaste!" Then they went on.

The boy said "Namche?"

"Yes."

"You will go to Everest? You have no family?"

Oliver said "I have a brother, and two sisters."

"You have no wife? No children?"

Oliver asked "Do you go to school…sometimes?"

"Yes…in Lukla."

Oliver said "All these mountains were under the sea…long ago."

The boy didn't answer.

At the other side, as he stepped ahead of the family, they smiled. Then the trail rose sharply again.

As Oliver climbed, he thought that the friendliness of the people was part of the music for him. And so was the land part of it; beautiful and dangerous as the sea.

About a hundred feet above the bridge, was the place he paused to look back, other times. When he got to it he didn't stop. As he passed he looked at his watch, while reminding himself that his body had six days dust, the kind that drifts up from India…so, he needed to get on to Namche, to order hot water for a shower.

Entering Namche, the trail goes sharply upward and toward the north. As he did, he stopped at a flat place between two rows of houses. It was where the Nepalis would be selling their goods.

Then he looked at the upper northwest corner of town, to where the Thame trail departed. He usually went there to sit, at the bend, high above the Bhote Kosi, which came down from the edge of Tibet.

Namche's half-bowl shape rested above the gorge.

He couldn't see the water, directly and far below, but could feel the power. It seemed very close…as did the mountain, across the way, which was a wall climbing to twenty thousand feet.

On houses near him, most of them one-story, and thatch-covered, the grass was weighted by rocks. The buildings were made of granite-like rock, hewn into shape, some with clay and white paint.

Prayer flags were still. Laundry was out to dry. The only person near was a royal Nepali Army corporal walking up the hill to a building above Oliver's head, to the right.

On the Everest trail, he moved up through the east side of town until he was higher than most of it. And the path was quite straight here, as it went toward the northeast edge. There were a few buildings beside the trail, at the upper part. One was his hotel, there to the right, with an outhouse at this end followed by a large courtyard in which expeditions sometimes put their tents. He couldn't see into the yard as he passed, it being higher than his head.

At the upper end of the hotel was a wooden arch, almost touching the trail. You needed to pass through it and walk around to the back of the building in order to get to the entrance.

Three westerners, two men and a woman, were standing near it, on the hotel side. The girl had black hair and very white skin, and looked familiar to him, but before he got closer she moved along the path to the inner corner. One of the men was waving his arm, telling her to continue to the entranceway, in the back.

After Oliver stepped into the arch, he nodded to the men then turned to look over the town. He hoped they didn't speak. He just wanted to observe.

"It's rather a dramatic sight, isn't it?" one of them said, in what Oliver thought was a New York City accent.

It was the dark-haired one, the shorter of the two. But he was about six feet tall. He continued to speak. "What is that square shape at the upper part of town...there in the middle? Are those rocks?"

"A reforestation area," Oliver said.

"Where is Khumjung? Hilary has a clinic there."

"Above the patch," said Oliver. "Over the hill…by twenty minutes, maybe. You pass through a forest."

"So…this is the trail to Everest," the man said, pointing to a spot just outside the archway. "We've sent in the lady to ask about how expensive this place is."

Oliver said "You can get a room for a couple bucks…or a bed for a dollar, in the big room."

The bigger man, a crew-cut blond, said "I was told to stay below." He pointed to the center of town. "That it's cheaper…and you can have a beer…and maybe meet a girl."

"This hotel is about empty," said Oliver. "I like to sit by the windows on the upper floor." He pointed. "And look out over the town."

"So, you've been here often," said the shorter man. "My name is Norm Ginsberg, and this is Bush."

After they shook hands, Bush said "My nickname is B…u…s…h. But my name is B…u…s…c…h."

Oliver asked "Are you old friends?"

"We met yesterday," said Norm. "Got drunk and formed a partnership. We're wanting to climb a twenty thousand foot mountain. About that size. Have you done that?"

"Yes."

Oliver considered asking if they had walked in from Jiri, for the workout, but he didn't,

As though reading part of his mind, Norm said "We flew in…to Lukla. No need for the walk from Jiri…I spent the summer climbing in Colorado, and Bush did the same in Oregon."

The girl yelled from the corner of the building, and told them to come.

"I sat beside her!" said Oliver. "Between Tokyo and Bangkok." And after the men reacted by staring, he added "My name is Oliver Faulkner. I'll see you inside."

Again alone, he leaned against the gateway, and half-attended to the main shopping lane, below. To this side of it was a level clearing, through which a solitary figure moved. It was a man with a red parka and large-brimmed hat of a light blue color.

The man went to shop, soon removing the hat and trying on others. And because he wondered about the man's age, he got his small binoculars. Yes, the hair was grey. He bought a dark blue baseball cap, but it was large, probably insulated. After opening the flaps and trying it that way, he tucked them in and put it on, and wore it.

Oliver lowered the binoculars, and rubbed his eyes, and said, aloud, "Is that my business? Should I be watching him?"

The shopping area was at the lower center of the bowl, and leading from the other side of it was a stone-walled path, angling up to the west corner, to the Thame trail.

Moving down between the walls of the path, which were about five feet high, was a caravan of yaks. Also, in the path and trying to climb out of it, was a man being helped by a young Tibetan who had run ahead of the yaks.

When the man got onto the wall, and sat, he removed his cap and rubbed his parka sleeve across his forehead. And Oliver saw white hair. He was older than the shopper.

Oliver said, aloud, "You shouldn't walk out, alone, here…at your age!"

A shrill voice came from behind him.

"Oliver…do you think my bones would break?"

It was the owner's youngest daughter, although grown to her early twenties.

"Shoree...my sweetie pie. I missed you!"

"Don't lie, Oliver!"

She began to walk toward the building.

"Did you come out to see me?"

At the corner she turned and said "Maybe I did! Maybe I love you!"

"Stop it!" he said. And as she disappeared "You're not thirteen...now...to say that. You're married!"

He attended to the town. Raising his binoculars, he saw that the old man was yet on the wall, and he, too, held a pair to his eyes, apparently studying the man in the archway.

Oliver lowered his eyes to the path near his feet. "This is where I lay down awhile."

He remembered taking the other trail, up to Thame... and looking north toward Nangpa La, the pass to Tibet. A river centered a valley with three towns in it, the first several miles away, the second so distant it seemed unreal, and the final one, at a curve northeast, barely perceptible, as a dot of life on the sea.

Then later, he was at Everest base camp and studied Lho La, and decided he could get over that into Tibet. But he left his crampons, and other gear, in Lobuche.

It seemed true for both trails that Tibet was not at the heart of the song.

Six times he had come here, as called...expecting wind to descend and stir the place to step.

Each time...being full of himself...he didn't wait for the wind. And so he would come again. Maybe."

CHAPTER THREE

Behind the hotel, and about four steps from it, was an eight-feet high rock wall, which restrained the hill and defined the alleyway. He touched it, having remembered the smooth surface, and looked along it to the courtyard, and outhouse.

No tents were in the yard.

He went inside and, climbing to the first floor of the living quarters, looked to his left through the hallway. Seeing padlocks on five of the eight rooms, he guessed that three of them were rented by the visitors he met outside, then he stepped to his right and opened the doors of the dormitory. It was empty.

At the top of the stairway, he hesitated...listening. To his left was the dining room's curtained entrane. He could hear the three visitors beyond it. Turning from it, he cleared his throat and pushed aside other curtains, at the doorway to the kitchen.

"Hello," he said. "May I enter?"

Inside, to his left, Shoree was sitting on a bench, and had one knee high, her foot resting flat. Showing an entire shapely leg, she was pretending not to know he was there, was looking through a window.

In the center of the room, at the whitened-clay cooking oven, the Sherpa lady, the woman of the house, was putting pieces of wood, some of them three feet long, onto red coals at the base of the main stove. And it seemed that she didn't hear him, because she now reached to a place above the stove for a large copper kettle. Without looking toward Shoree, she said, gently, but firmly, "Get water!"

After a glance-attend to Oliver, she put down the kettle and readjusted firewood. Then she gazed to the side and upward, as though remembering.

As Shoree picked up the kettle and went across for water, she said "I told you he was here!"

"Ah...hello," said the lady, beginning to wipe her hands on a towel hooked to her waist, and stepping toward him. She hugged him, and had never done that. "I have a room for you."

She got a key from a wall-hook beyond where Shoree had been sitting, and led him through the curtains.

In the hallway, below, she went to the third door on the left and, after opening it, handed him the key.

As he entered, she asked "Would you like tea?...and a basin of hot water? I can have Shoree bring it."

Taking off his packsack he leaned it against the bunk on his left. He would sleep on the other. Then he was pleased to be facing the rock wall and the hill. There was the schoolhouse...a couple hundred feet up the grassy slope.

"Not much snow," he said to the lady. "Only a line of it near the schoolhouse. No…I'll go upstairs for tea. To the restaurant." They had agreed, once, that if others were in the hotel he wouldn't sit with her in the kitchen. "Later, will you make me hot water for a shower?"

In the restaurant, the men sat at a long table near the windows at the town side. Their backs were to the glass, and Norm had a map laid out.

Norm, who was closest to the kitchen, said "Hello! Come sit with us!"

Rather than be across from them, Oliver sat beside Norm, then turned his chair, slightly, to better see the outside view.

Walking up the trail, and almost to the courtyard was the grey-haired man with the red parka. And not far behind him was the smaller, white-haired man.

Norm said, "We're planning to spend today and tomorrow here, then head north to Lobuche. Three mountains are right there…all about twenty thousand feet. Did I tell you my name is Notm?"

"Yes."

Norm jerked his head toward Bush. "He'll anchor the expedition. And why not? He's more man than we are."

"Perhaps…but speak for yourself!" said Oliver.

Norm continued as though he didn't hear that. "What did you say your name is?…Oliver? You're about my size. Where do you live?"

"The Aleutians." And when neither man responded, he added "I'm from New Hampshire, but I went to Alaska ten years ago. I'm a fisherman."

Norm said "This is assuming you're coming with us. Which Bush and I have agreed to." He leaned toward Oliver. "We need you to guide us."

"What did I agree to?" asked Bush.

Oliver said "I haven't climbed any of the mountains you chose. I would guess that Lobuche East is not difficult. You only need to be careful…and have crampons, and a supporting shaft. Yes…you should have an ice axe."

"So. Are you with us?" asked Norm. "We want someone along who has experience with altitude."

"No. But thanks for asking."

Both Norm and Bush looked at him blankly. Apparently they expected a "Yes".

He said "In a couple days you'll be in Pheriche. A handful of houses. They have a clinic, and someone gives a talk about altitude problems."

Bush said, in a high-pitched voice, "I think maybe you don't want to climb with us."

"I have other plans, Bush. My own high place is calling. A mountain beyond a pass called Changri." Which only called to him at this moment. "I saw it on a map…just yesterday. Also…I lost five hundred dollars while traveling to Nepal. It was stolen. So, my time is limited."

Oliver now decided he'd go, at least, to Changri La.

Norm said "Could you take us to your mountain? Which one is it?"

"It isn't named on your map. Look for Gyubanare Glacier. The mountain is west of Chumbu."

"And you've been there?" asked Norm.

"No. I've looked that way...west from Kala Patar. That's where the trail turns east to Everest. I looked out across the glacier."

"How will you know where to go?" Bush asked.

"Why should you lead us?"

Oliver said "Why would I want you to follow me?" He sighed. "I have a topographical map. But...I'm short of money, so I'll be doing mine in ten or eleven days...maybe. From here to the mountain and back. Or...wherever I go. Probably you don't want to rush."

"You wouldn't need to rush," said Norm. "If we paid you the three hundred dollars you lost. We have two more people coming from Lukla. Marlaine's sister is coming, and some guy she met there. That would be five. Sixty dollars each. Can you wait until tomorrow to decide?"

Bush said "I've got to think about it!"

"You can afford it!" said Norm.

Oliver said "Yes. I'll wait until I meet the other two." He looked at Bush. "I'm not thinking I'm better than anybody. It's just that at this time I don't know what I want. I feel empty."

Bush smiled, and said "It could be that you're full of yourself...now."

From that response, Oliver figured Bush to be smarter than he had taken him to be, and maybe not that bad of a person underneath.

"I don't know where I'm going, Bush. I'm waiting. It has nothing to do with thinking I ought to be alone."

Oliver returned to his room. It was cold, so he took off his boots and got into his bag. He slept.

When he awoke it was dark and, because he didn't get candles from the Sherpa lady, he felt in the pack for his flashlight. Then, seeing it was dinnertime, he put on his boots, and departed...locking the door behind him.

As he went up the stairs he hoped his new friends would speak of things other than a climb. Maybe he'd tell Norm it was his girlfriend who stole the money. He stopped, and laughed. "Three...? What happened to five hundred?"

Pulling open the curtain, he saw Norm and Bush at the same table, as earlier, but on the inner side, away from the windows. The girl was sitting between the two. Beyond them, was a smaller table near the south wall, and at one end of it, sat the man with the red parka, the grey-haired man.

This older man seemed to be sleeping. He was hunched forward, and his head was down.

Nearly touching his back was another table. At the end away from the grey-haired man, sat the man with white hair.

As Oliver entered and went to Norm's table, the girl was staring at him.

"Hello," he said to her. He extended his hand. "We sat together on the flight from Tokyo to Bangkok."

Shaking his hand, she said "My sister will be here tomorrow. She'll take care of you."

To Oliver, what she meant was clear. Her sister would pay him. His money had been in three places, one being in a mid-thigh pocket, toward her. It had contained five hundred dollars.

Bush said "I've known you longer than he has, Marlaine. Maybe your sister can take care of me."

Oliver was yet holding her hand. They attended to one another, silently, to convey understanding. But the sound of Bush's words cut in.

Marlaine said, angrily, "I didn't mean that!"

She let go of Oliver's hand and faced the table, looking down at it.

Oliver glanced at Norm, then got up, stepping away from the bench. "I need to visit that white-haired man."

Norm responded in a commanding voice. "Make it only a minute, please! I've got to make decisions."

Oliver went to the old man.

"I know you!" he said.

The man smiled and held forward his hand, which Oliver grasped.

"Sure you do, Oliver! You've seen me in Unalaska for twenty years. You have a metal skiff, with a small cabin forward…about a twenty-five footer…and you pulled alongside me one day at Cape Cheerful. You were fishing cod. Yeh…I remember. You had three jigging machines."

Oliver said "You were running that round bottom, tunnel-stern boat, with the high cabin. As you went rolling west, I could see that it was hard to steer. Where were you heading…Makushin Bay?"

"Yeh…I thought about oyster farming…was wanting a protected cove away from town. Isn't it funny?" The old man smiled. "When we meet officially, it's here, where I didn't think I'd ever be. A friend of mine got a free trip but couldn't make it, so he gave it to me. I don't belong here!"

Oliver said "An old salt like you…in the Himalayas. Who would have thought it? My name is Oliver Faulkner."

"I know! I'm Little John, but I'm getting too old to be called that…just call me John. John Finn."

"Sure!" Oliver smiled. I need to get back to the other table. They asked me to guide them to a mountain above Lobuche. I wouldn't bother, but I lost money, and that fellow said they would pay me. John…maybe you do belong here…these mountains were once under the sea."

"Yeh…today I was near a wall made of beach rock. How high is this town?"

"Eleven…twelve thousand."

"John said "I've been at sea level more than seventy years…and I'm sitting here? No!...that's not true, I was a tail gunner on a B25 in the second world war…but I never thought I'd walk up into the air, on purpose." And as Oliver began to step away, John added "You better come back soon! The only other person I talk to is the boss of the house, the beautiful Sherpa lady."

John now waved his hand to Oliver, calling back, and he began to whisper.

"This gentleman near me, at the other table," John pointed. "Is he dead? I saw him shopping, today, but he hasn't moved for an hour."

At that moment the grey-haired man took a deep breath.

Oliver went to Norm's table and sat.

Norm said "Marlaine got a note from her sister. She'll be here early…with that man she met. She says she doesn't like him…can't recommend him. It's OK, we'll have four to pay you. So, I need to know…soon as she gets here, whether or not you'll guide us. I'll be the boss, but that's understood! Marlaine…" Norm had already turned away from him. "Let's have dinner."

Marlaine gathered the menu books of Norm and Bush, and went quickly to the curtains.

Oliver thought it was too bad she was being servile to a man who seemed to love having servants. ~~The~~ THEN he remembered the strength she showed when standing alone to face her thievery. It could be that only parts of her were childlike, wanting the proper hand. He hoped Norm would be the right one.

As to his own path, he was deciding to have nothing to do with Norm and Bush. That's what he'd say in the morning. And meeting Marlaine's sister wouldn't change a thing.

Now the Sherpa lady came in, and Shoree, each with notebook and pen. Shoree put hers before him.

He said "Shoree…sweetie pie…I already filled out this one." He handed her a notebook.

Smiling, she got closer to him and whispered. "I'll knock on your door…in the dark."

He whispered "No!...don't! I'll be here only a few days. And…"

She sharply drew in her breath, and pulled away her head. Without another word she went to John's table and handed the menu to her mother.

Both ladies attended to the old man awhile, and often all three were speaking at once. Then the mother went to the man wearing the blue parka, and when she rested a hand on his shoulder, and leaned close to speak to him, he came back to this place. He moved his whole body as though testing his muscles, and looked up at her. She handed him a notebook.

Norm said "Hey…Oliver. Tomorrow morning I'll hire three porters." Then he grasped Marlaine's hand and, without looking at her, pulled her to him. "One each for the girls and one for you. Of course, maybe you don't want one, but I know Bush and I are strong enough to carry our load...and Marlaine's sister is arriving with a young man. She doesn't like him, but I might."

Oliver laughed. "How old are you, Norm?"

"Twenty five."

"My being thirty five is serving your purpose. But, if I want a porter I'll hire one."

"Just trying to be helpful!" Norm snorted, looking at Marlaine. "I'm the one with the money."

Shoree had left the room. She now brought a dish of rice for Oliver. He said "Will you please put it by the old man. I'll eat with him."

Norm said "I might have more to say."

"Say it in the morning," Oliver answered, standing. "After those people arrive."

"I'm the boss! Said Norm, grasping at Oliver's sleeve. "You've got to know that!"

Oliver knocked away the hand. "Then use your head better!"

He stood beside Norm, wondering if he should end this tie now, rather than in the morning. What could possibly happen then to change anything?

His interest went to the table of the man with the blue parka. The Sherpa lady had food for him.

Speaking loudly, the lady said "Mr. Barton...how are you tonight?"

"Fine, thanks! I got a chill...maybe I'll put on my parka. Will you have hot coals in the bucket?"

"Yes, I will!" she answered. "But you already do." She lowered her voice. "You have it on."

Mr. Barton looked down. "Oh, yes…I can see that."

John said "You're cold because you haven't breathed for an hour. Don't scare me that way! I thought you were dead. My name is John Finn."

Mr. Barton turned to look. Then he smiled. "Hello, I'm Greg Barton."

The lady brought what remained on the tray to John, who said "You beautiful lady. You remembered that I can't eat green peppers."

"There's none," she said. "Potato, onion, tomato, delicious yak meat…that I beat with my hammer, a half hour, just for you."

She stepped toward the kitchen.

Bush said "We ordered before they did!"

The lady answered, gently, "You're young, you can wait a minute."

Bush spoke loudly to Greg Barton. "Have you been sleeping?"

Barton looked at Bush and spoke easily. "In a way. I think my spirit, or soul, was apart from my body mind. But I'm not certain. Maybe I'm only imagining it."

Marlaine said "Was your body that much out of control?"

"No! My body knew what it was doing."

John Finn said "When I die, my body will go to sleep, and my soul will go fishing. I already know that." He laughed.

Greg Barton took off his parka, and laughed along with John.

"What's so funny?" Bush said. "How old are you?"

He asked it of Barton.

"I'm sixty five."

"You've been here awhile. How long?" Bush asked. "Everybody else just arrived."

"I've been here a week."

"What's an old fart like you doin' up here, where young people belong?"

Oliver's body tensed. Adrenaline rushed through.

Little John said, in a voice louder than Bush's, "I'm seventy five. One more crack from you…and I'll make you pay for it!"

"Oh, will you!" said Bush, turning his chair as he faced John, and smiling as he did so.

John got up and, holding his chair in one hand, walked to Bush. He raised it, until it was shoulder high.

Bush said "Don't try it! You don't hardly come up to my chest. I can take that chair away."

Oliver got up.

Now Bush was holding his arm in front of himself as though he didn't quite believe his own words.

"Let's see you do it!" said John, now holding it over his head. "Say something about my age…or his!"

Norm spoke strongly to Bush. "If you fight with them, you're off my expedition."

Bush turned away from John and held his hands palm up and open. "I'm not fighting."

"You better apologize to them," Norm said.

Bush shrugged his shoulders. "I apologize."

Oliver sat.

Now Bush said "Why did grampa get so mad?"

CHAPTER FOUR

When Oliver stepped through the gateway and began moving down the trail, it was late in a blue-sky morning. The night had been cold, and the sun, just up, put a glisten to the mud. Bells of a yak train tinkled crisply, right there, ascending, so he moved to the very outside. To the Nepalese he said "Namaste."

Norm, Bush, and Marlaine were farther down the hill, and were descending. They stopped, and greeted two newly arrived trekkers, one a female and the other a tall blond man, of very short hair. Marlaine was hugging the girl.

As he watched, everyone but the blond man continued downward, but where the trail turned to the right and descended sharply toward the center of town, Marlaine put an arm around her sister's shoulders and pointed up the hill. Then they stopped, again, apparently to wait for him to go down.

The blond man stepped upward strongly, and briskly, but with left hand at his side, holding open his jacket, while the other hand carried a walking stick which he slapped, hard, against his leg.

The man raised his head and saw that he was being attended to, after which he slowed his pace, and held his head down and to the side, as though wanting to give the impression he could barely hold it up. Then he looked again, and smiled broadly. But when he got to Oliver he smiled weakly, as though exasperated.

"Oliver Faulkner?" the man said, in a moderate tone. He held forward his hand, which Oliver took. "I'm Curt Monahan. I walked up with the girl from Connecticut, and that's where I'm from. They asked me to join your climb, and said it would take three weeks and cost eighty bucks. What I have to do won't take that long. Now...I've got a headache...a big one. So I won't stop to chat."

The man nodded...and, slowly, sighingly, moved onward a step.

Oliver remembered Norm calling him a young man, meaning, for him, "twenties". Obviously he wasn't that. But, perhaps, more importantly, he seemed to be strong and pretending not to be.

"Did you fly in?" Oliver asked. Then he added "It's all right...you don't need to answer."

Curt stopped, and half turned. He was looking at the ground. "I flew into Lukla yesterday. Had a helluva headache last night."

"How long did it last?"

Curt was wanting to move on. He took a step, but then answered. "An hour or two."

"And it didn't hurt again until now?" Oliver asked.

"Just before you got to me."

"Yeh...that's correct!" Curt stepped ahead again, with some strength. "So I'm going for a nap."

As Oliver watched him move away, he thought "He's a liar...but I don't know that it's harmful. And I have no plans to find out."

As he began to descend toward the others, he attended to Marlaine's sister...a strawberryish blond.

She wore a dark blue parka, unzipped, and being held apart because she had hands on hips. Her sweater was brown and apparently thin, as it dropped away from her chin.

Oliver said, aloud, to himself, "I think of fresh strawberries...but there's only a dash of red in her hair it seems. I...why do I feel space curving her way? I better eat...and hold on. What the devil...I..."

She lowered her sunglasses.

"Good!" he said. "That stirs things. What? Oh, yes, my next step. I..."

When he got to her he looked deeply into her eyes...and she into his.

Awhile.

Between thoughts, where one is "loving only", how does time pass for the soul?

Then he could hear music.

"Look!" Marlaine said. "They're dancing!...and singing! Down near the shopping area, at the flat ground. There's a group of Nepali women in a circle."

Norm said "That instrument they're playing...the little violin...is called a gaini. Let's go down."

Oliver said to the girl "My name is Oliver Faulkner. You have gentle skin...and should wear cream."

Reaching into his pocket, he brought out a small tin. "Of this kind."

"I'm Molly Firfer." She smiled, then brought forth a white glass container. "I have some of this on." She touched her cheek.

He touched it, too. He did it gently, with his finger-tips. "That cream has water in it, and could freeze to your soft skin. What did you say your name is?"

"Molly."

He placed his opened hand against her cheek. "I'll give you mine."

She said "I have something for you."

He waited.

After awhile she said "What did you say?"

He said "Your eyes have a bit of brownish gold…and green. Is that what this is about?"

"It's because they're deep blue," she said.

"I'll say this, Molly…I seem to be happy here."

"Yes."

Their names were being called, from far away.

He put his hands on her shoulders, then removed them. He cleared his throat.

She said "I need to know where you're from." Then she laughed.

"New Hampshire!" he said, raising his shoulders. "In the river beds the wind, with shadows on dry stones."

"Too bad!" she said.

"It's a line from a poem I wrote. A long time ago." He scratched his cheek. "It popped into my head."

"I know. I was born in Groton, Connecticut."

He said "And so…?"

"But I lived in Concord, New Hampshire…for a year. In my early twenties."

"It must be fresh in your mind," he said, smiling.

She smiled, too, and holding her hand flat, was about to answer, but didn't. She blushed.

He said, gently, "Both of us have lowered shields."

She said "And in this circle stand trembling…the ancient rules secure, yet offering eternal victory or defeat."

He asked "Did you read that somewhere?"

"Yes…in a poem I wrote."

"Molly…our hearts made this playing field. It's one to one."

"Oliver, I've been three years in Seattle. Oh!...I'm to give you five hundred dollars."

"She steals, and you return it?"

"Sometimes." She got a roll of money from an inside jacket pocket and handed it to him. "Marlaine said to tell you "Thanks for understanding". Where do you live now?"

"Alaska…the Aleutians. That chain of islands. I taught English in a little school there. Now I'm a fisherman. I jig for cod."

"Oliver, you say our hearts made this field. But, is fate the greater builder? Other men have said "Hello" to me… but maybe I wasn't there. I was here. I…"

He said "According to Molly's choices…forms her carpet. At the bridge, tomorrow is another day. You and I will tread on a tiger's tail…and be made one heart…or not."

They walked down to the crowd, which was yet in the open space, and watched the girls again join hands. One sang in a pleasant, strong voice and, when she finished, the others answered, in chorus.

After being there awhile they went to the shopping lane, and she got an ice axe. In the back of the shop he found two brass-tipped walking staffs. They were light but stout, and could bend, slightly, under his weight without seeming to be unduly stressed. He bought them and gave the shorter one to her. Then he made her exchange the axe for a lighter one, and he got one for himself.

At that place, he found crampons made to be worn with any type of boot, so he bought two pairs.

The owner, an older Sherpa man, was expression-less during the shopping, but when he gave Oliver change he smiled and said "I miss it. Have a nice time."

They went on, looking into the buildings, most of them two-story, with the bottom floor open to the lane.

Leaving the shops, on the other side of town they got on the Thame trail and walked up between the shoulder-high walls, where John Finn encountered the yak train. The hard mud was slippery, but large rocks were there to walk on and had been placed carefully, through the centuries.

Their names were being called from the direction of the center of the basin. Marlaine, with the others, was on a trail which touched theirs.

"We're climbing to where they planted trees." Said Marlaine, pointing. "Then maybe up to Khumjung. Come with us."

Molly looked at Oliver.

"Go ahead!" he said, "If you want to. I don't."

Molly said "Oliver and I have business to discuss. I'll be at the hotel by noon."

Between the two girls, where the trails joined, was a raised, wooden barrier to block pack animals. Shaped prism-like, and a couple feet high at its highest, it had spaces to catch hoofed legs. Molly stepped onto it, reaching for her sister's hand.

Molly asked "Are you having a good time?"

Oliver guessed that Molly was the younger by four or five years…but she seemed to be the more self-assured.

"I'm all right," answered Marlaine, taking Molly's hand. Then…both let go and began to turn away.

As Molly looked down at her feet, to have a safe step, Bush reached out and grasped her parka, preventing her from moving.

"I'll buy you lunch," Bush said, grinning.

"No!...you won't!" said Molly.

Oliver stepped onto the crossing.

Marlaine yelled "Norm, tell him to let go!"

But Bush had already done that, so Oliver needed only to support Molly, to keep her from falling.

When they were again standing on the Thame trail, the three others were departing, probably at the insistence of Marlaine; and, after a few steps, Norm looked at Bush, and spoke, and Bush shrugged his shoulders.

Holding Molly's hand, Oliver stepped upward in the trail, onto a flat rock, and she followed him.

"This is the Thame trail," he said. "And the old trading route to Tibet. We'll walk up to the northwest edge. There." He pointed. "To the corner of the bowl. Want to?"

"Yes, Oliver…I want to."

In awhile they came to that place which was almost entirely around the bend from town, and was high above the river.

He sat on the outside, and she leaned against him.

She said "I'm trying to see the water. Is that the Bhote Kosi?"

"Yes. If you look far down the valley…see where it turns directly south? You can tell from the contour above it, that it's joined, there, by the one coming down from the north…the Dudh Kosi."

She said "Through the valley running north on the other side of Namche." With a sigh, she added "I was on the bridge awhile…watching the water move away."

"What did you think of?"

"I sort of felt the carpet…as you say. Kathmandu and Bangkok, and Tokyo and Groton, Connecticut. I was at the University of New Hampshire a year, before Marlaine moved to Seattle. I followed her. I've been working in a clothing store. I applied to beauty school, for being a hair stylist. Later, maybe I'll do that."

"Did you think that…on the bridge?"

"No…I was just there…on the bridge."

"Why did you leave the University?"

"It seemed pointless…my being there. But…I might have majored in English Literature. I like to read."

"I got a degree in that…from there…but I'm a fisherman. My recent thought was to be a helicopter pilot." He laughed. "And yet…when you were ten, and as you paused on the bridge below Namche…Molly was Molly. You were the pearl in the night."

"What do you mean by that?"

He put his arms around her and, pulling her in, kissed her on the lips.

"If someone described your smile, at ten, it would do for Molly."

He slid his fingers through her hair.

"Oliver, I feel dusty from my trip. Will you take me to the hotel...so I can settle in?"

He got up, and she quickly followed. Then...without speaking, but with a lightness in their step, they went back down the trail.

When they got to the shopping lane, he took her hand into his. The man who sold them the walking sticks said "Hello" and smiled.

At the place in the trail where they first met, Oliver stopped and put his arm around her, inside her parka. His cheek was against hers.

"I like the feel of your hair on my face," he said.

They were that way for a minute, then he kissed her.

She said "We made the choices to get here. But...maybe I could feel it yesterday on the bridge. I felt empty, but happy. Oliver...where is the tiger's tail?"

"Molly, if we don't hide from life...it's around every bend."

CHAPTER FIVE

Her door was directly across from his. As he stood near it he heard her yawning and stretching. "Molly, are you ready for lunch? Or…maybe I'll come into your room."

At that he got very excited.

"No! Oliver, I won't have a shower until later. It's a small room, is what I meant. I'll be up in a few minutes. Will you order me toast?…and a couple boiled eggs."

So he went up the stairs. At the top…he said, aloud, "I'd call that magic."

Shoree came from the kitchen, and saw the change…in the contour of his pants.

"Did you want to kidnap me?" she said.

When he entered the dining room, she was by his side, and had her hand on his arm.

There was a group of five newcomers against the east wall, to his left; otherwise, the situation was as expected. John Finn was in his place, and Greg Barton. At the table facing town, there was Norm, sitting nearest to the curtains, and then Marlaine, Bush and Curt.

Bush and Curt were of a physical match in height, and so were taller than everyone else, but Bush's hair was a bit longer, and he was heavier. They had turned on the bench to face one another, and were conversing. Now Curt looked over Bush's shoulder at him, and then at Shoree…where his eyes remained.

John Finn was beckoning, with a wave of his hand.

Oliver spoke to Shoree, who yet touched him. "Shoree, why is it that a Sherpani as beautiful as you, has a husband far away?"

She left his side, with her head down, and asked Norm for his menu.

From behind Oliver the Sherpa lady spoke, softly. "Shoree has a husband who beats her…and a boy, two years old, who is in Tyangboche."

Oliver went to John's table.

"Sit here!" John said. "Eat with me!"

"I will…but I need to talk with Norm first. John…I met a girl. I'll introduce you. Her name is Molly."

"I know. I saw you with her. The strawberry blond. The prettiest western girl I've seen for a long while. But…why did you have this Sherpa girl at your side?"

"We're old friends. I knew her from when she was twelve. She grabbed my arm on the way in."

"I think that blond man…the new one, talking to your pal Norm, has decided to take her away from you…even if she isn't yours."

Shoree had arrived at Curt, who had his hand on her side. She stepped away, and returned to the kitchen.

"Oliver, I think Norm wants to see you. He's looking this way. Have you decided to not guide his expedition?"

"I'm on it...for a couple weeks."

When Oliver began to step away, John called him back, as he did earlier, and again whispered. "Mr. Barton is eating and drinking, and he said "Hello" to me...but he isn't here."

He went to Norm's table.

"Mr. Faulkner," said Norm. "I believe it's set for leaving in the morning. We have five...including the new one, Curt."

Oliver said "I guess Molly can tolerate him, if they walked up together from Lukla."

"They didn't," said Norm. "They met again at the bottom of this town. Marlaine told me. But I find him acceptable."

"I'm in," said Oliver. "But Norm...as the leader, you've got to keep Bush in order. I won't have him bothering Molly."

"I'll do that, Oliver. And today I'll get porters. Have any recommendations?"

Norm was being reasonable. Probably his tension eased when he saw that his guide was not interested in Marlaine.

"I'd go through the Sherpa lady, Norm. She can bring in three or four porters and one of them can be paid extra for taking charge, and one can be a cook if we spend much time above Lobuche. But...we'll need to feed them, and provide a tent. Maybe more."

Shoree's grandmother, short and thin, came in and recognized Oliver. She shrieked, and began walking around the wood-burner heater in an exaggerated side to side sway.

She said "All the girls are bowlegged now."

Oliver said to Shoree "That's who you learned your tricks from."

Shoree looked at him but didn't smile.

"Namaste", Oliver said to the old lady. "It's nice to see you."

The old lady put her hands together, and held them above her forehead. "Namaste" she said.

When Molly came in he took her to John, and presented her. "John and I know one another…from before. He's a fisherman. An old timer."

"Where's your brown sweater…you look so pretty in?" asked John, shaking hands with her. "But…it's O.K. for you to wear the same color as Oliver."

She was wearing a turtleneck of a finer texture than his, but also black.

"It's a coincidence," she said. "In the same way as you and Oliver being here, together. Two fisherman from the same little town in Alaska."

John said "You better bring her home with you."

They went to the other table, where Molly sat beside Norm, and he next to her, at the end.

She exchanged words with her sister, and a touch of hands, behind Norm's back. Oliver attended to it.

"Menu…?" Shoree was asking, and was beside him.'

After he wrote down what he wanted, and handed it to her, he said "Sorry I teased you. You have a husband who is bad?"

She didn't smile at that.

"You have a little boy in Tyangboche? When I go there I can bring him something from you. Maybe tomorrow."

She smiled…and nodded…then went into the kitchen.

As he turned to face the table, suddenly Bush was behind him, so he looked up. The man ignored him; he was studying Molly.

Molly looked up.

Bush put his right leg over the bench and, facing Molly, forced himself between them. In doing so, his back came hard against Oliver's left shoulder.

"You're the girl for me!" Bush snorted. "I'll buy you dinner!"

Oliver got up.

Without hesitation, he reached around, and rapped his hand against Bush's nose. When the man's entire upper body jerked backward, Oliver kept him moving that way. By grasping his shirt with both hands he threw him to the floor.

Bush raised himself to his hands and knees, and with head down, bellowed "You'll pay for that! I'll flatten your shit-ass head!"

At that, Oliver quickly grasped Bush's shirt and his crotch, raising him several inches from the floor, and walked him to the curtains. Passing through, he continued to the edge of the stairs, and propelled him hard as he could, far out as he could.

Most of the movement had been done by Bush's fighting to stand upright, so he didn't go very far out. He tumbled five or six steps.

When Oliver began descending, Bush was on his left side, right hand on the floor, and was looking toward the bottom of the stairs.

"Outside!" said Oliver, having stopped one step above, "You're not hurt!"

Bush reached for him, but he avoided contact by stepping upward. Now Bush got up by bracing himself against the left wall. He faced it. So, Oliver was able to pass.

He went down the stairs, through the entrance and into the yard. He walked the few steps to the wall, and looked at it. It seemed higher than he remembered. It was at least nine feet high. After touching it, he turned to face the doorway.

Upstairs...he did what he had to do. But...the pit of his stomach knew that in a few seconds a man six inches taller and seventy pounds heavier would burst through the door.

Oliver figured that...probably...he was about to get his ass kicked.

Now Bush came through the door and, after it slammed shut, stood glaring at him. Then he grinned, broadly. "After I kick your ass...I'll make you eat yak shit...and then you won't think you're so smart."

Oliver wanted this to end.

Bush charged across the open space, pivoted his body quite far to his right, and readied a sweeping punch. Obviously he thought this fight would be short.

As Bush was swinging, Oliver stepped away a bit, then delivered a fairly hard left and right to the side of that big chin. And because the man's next move was a sweeping left, Oliver gave him two more to the other side.

Bush stood fully upright and gathered his fists, bringing them to a position close to his chest.

It already seemed to Oliver that this powerful man would not be able to move fast enough to hit him, unless he, himself, didn't attend fully. So...he attended. He went under Bush's arms, delivering his right to the ribs. Then he bobbed to the left, moved to the right, his feet yet planted firmly, and went to the chin somewhat harder than before.

Immediately he again brought the right to the same place, stiffly.

All of which seemed to have no physical effect on Bush, except to begin changing him from being angry to being in a rage. His face was turning redder.

Bush charged again, evidently wanting to trap him against the wall. And…as Oliver attended to this, he had already stepped backward until he was touching it.

He snapped a left to Bush's chin, and a right; then as his own back bounced off the wall, drove a right, again, into the ribs. All seemingly for nothing.

He knew that if Bush got a hold of any part of him, particularly his clothing, and restrained him, then he would get hit. So, perhaps helped by this thought, he leaped aside, to his left, getting away from Bush and the wall.

Oliver became aware that windows of the building were open, and people were watching. This disgusted him, feeling there was only one way he could defeat Bush, and that was by almost over-loading his effort or by getting vicious.

His sharp, stiffly moderate punches had done nothing to stop Bush. So…wanting to finish this…he TRIED to hit him hard as he could, on the side of the chin. It didn't land there. Bush had lowered his head, slightly, so the fist hit higher, well above the eye.

Which hurt Oliver's hand. He remembered that his brother, Jim, when they were kids, had broken several knuckles by doing that.

And the punch seemed to not bother Bush.

Bush threw another sweeping right, and Oliver's boot got caught on a rock. There was a tiny delay in movement, and this allowed Bush to make contact.

Bush missed with the right, but he made the step forward he couldn't do before, and delivered a heavy left. It was a blow which came with the shoulder behind it, and picked Oliver off his feet.

It could have ended the fight. But...because Oliver had twisted his body sharply to the left, he got hit high on the back, above the ribs; and Bush's arm was about four inches beyond its center of power. So, although the blow hurt, he was able to get quickly up.

There was a look of brutal determination on Bush's face, and the reason Oliver attended fully to it, was due to his own lack of hate. He himself...was only doing what he needed to do. But he knew he might die doing it, if he didn't change his manner.

Oliver decided to press a button...to not hold back. He would go unobstructedly ahead, as he did when he was little and drove his straightened hand hard into the earth, penetrating far without injury.

But he didn't press it. The punch he threw, aimed for Bush's throat, was not a stepping up of power, but a deadly trick, and in mid-thrust he changed his mind. He had straightened his hand. Now he bent his fingers.

In that changing, he missed.

Suddenly there were three yaks, and a man leading them, the bells sounding first; and when they were around the north corner the man's whip was cracking and was whistling.

Bush went to the wall, Oliver to the building.

Molly stepped from the doorway. She yelled "Stop it!"

Now the yaks were right there, and the bells and the whip; and there was the smell of the animals and the feel of their strength. And then they were past.

Bush began to cross the space…face contorted, mouth and eyes wide, fists clenched and raised, one being above his shoulder.

This time Oliver didn't miss. Although he clenched his fist, he powered it beneath the chin. Which made Bush stop and be still. It made the man's eyes get smaller and took away the brutal opened mouth. Then it made him step backward one step, toward the yak's rear ends.

Now Oliver pressed a button…moving into a freer place. He hit Bush four or five times with nearly unobstructed power and placement. And Bush went down and didn't move, until he rolled onto his back, with opened mouth, seemingly at peace.

Oliver saw Molly disappear into the building.

He felt sick, and wondered if he'd vomit, but the feeling passed. He kneeled beside Bush, whose eyes were open and had just fluttered half a dozen times.

Oliver took off his own jacket and, rolling it up, put it under Bush's head.

Now Bush fully regained consciousness. He jerked his head upward several inches and looked around, and up at Oliver.

"The fight is done, Bush."

Bush raised his hand to his head, touching his fingers, lightly, to a place at his left temple. Then he felt his throat.

"Bush…let's go inside! You can wash your face. I'll ask the lady for hot water."

"Yeh...good idea!" and Bush reached for Oliver's shoulder as he began to get up.

He and Bush went together to the entrance, where Molly was holding open the door. But when he touched its latch she went quickly up the stairs.

In the kitchen, the Sherpa lady, the grandmother, and Molly stood at the stoves, staring at the fire.

He cleared his throat. "Excuse me!"

"Yes..." said Molly. "You should get the bad stuff out of your throat!"

"Can we have water and soap?"

There was a small table by the windows, near the bench Shoree was at earlier. Bush shuffled to it, and sat. He folded his hands and looked toward the women.

Quietely, the Sherpa lady said "You can put cold water in this!" She gave a large metal bowl to Molly, and nodded toward a covered porcelain container.

The he watched Bush hold a soaked washcloth against his swollen, red face, in different places, the darkest red being under the chin.

Oliver's hand was swollen on the back, but he was able to flex it.

Molly said, as she was walking to the curtains, "They lately cloned a sheep in Scotland." She stopped, made her hands into fists and held them against her hips. So...who needs men?" After which she disappeared.

He went into the hallway, but she was not in sight.

John Finn, who had parted the curtains of the dining room entrance, looked at him, then at the stairs, and stepped in that direction. Obviously, he was angry.

Now John turned, and faced him.

"You have a lot of ability…but when you knock down a man that big…the way you did in here…" He jerked his thumb toward the dining room. "You've got to keep him down! You give him the works, right then…and get it done with. This "fair chance" bullshit will get you killed. Although…" John now softened. "I did it, too, more than once…and considering what happened outside…well…doing it in the dining room would have been messy…I…anyway, I'm glad you're all right."

"John…I did what I had to do…between Bush and I… alone. Also…if I hit him when he was down, it would have been cowardly. And there was no thought of defeat."

John said "You mean you had "good" on your side?"

"I defended Molly and me…and proper conduct. Courage is what that necessity allows."

"You didn't lose your temper?"

"I…yeh, sure. But I confronted what he did…not what he is." He laughed. "Most of the time. Anyway, John, I tripped on a rock."

Oliver, that's when Molly flew down the steps. The way the sound echoes off that wall…that punch from Bush was loud. Did he hit you in the back? It seemed like you were finished. You didn't see my leg out the window? I was gonna clobber him."

"With what?"

John snorted. "It's different here! Where would I find a two by four….or an anchor chain? But I would have found something."

"John…I love Molly."

"That was quick!" said John. Now he whispered, "Listen! When you dropped Bush, that's when Curt left."

"So...?"

"So you should have seen him during the fight. Like he was having sex...or in training to be a clown. I mean it!... he looked crazy. And when he turned away from the scene, and toward me, he didn't see me. He was seeing something else...and his eyes and mouth were wide, and he had tears. Then he came back, regained awareness of me and the room. And he departed. That's it."

Oliver said "We can keep our eye on him."

"But..." John continued, "He rushed up here to the dining room, so I went to the edge of the hallway, below. Then he came out...couldn't have been in here more than ten seconds...and hurried down the stairs. He went to his room, got his parka and packsack, and departed the hotel."

"Maybe he needed to be calmed," Oliver said, glancing at his watch. "It's early afternoon. Maybe he wants to hike awhile. What are you making of it?"

"Oliver, there's a book on the table, where you sit. He put it there. And I'm just telling ya...because he's crazy. He has some kind of scheme that he brought up the hill with him. I..." John sighed and shrugged his shoulders. "But what do I know...an old fisherman in the mountains. Yeh...I've been wrong plenty of times. I'll see you at dinner. You better talk to Molly."

Now the Sherpa lady came from the kitchen. She said "If you see Shoree, please tell her to come. I need her!"

He went down and knocked on Molly's door, and there was no response. It was quiet within.

"Molly, can you hear me?"

There was no answer.

"Don't be mad! I had to stop him from bothering you, and he insulted me. I did something about it. Molly...?"

"What?"

"Why are you so upset?"

When she answered...she was nearer to the door. "Because the lady would have kicked him out, if you asked. And if he didn't go, she could have got the army to do it." Molly was silent for a long moment. "I thought he killed you...he hit you so hard!"

"Yeh...John said I should've stopped Bush, earlier, in the dining room. But, Molly, I wanted to give him a fair chance. Sure...I gave him a chance to scramble my brains."

"He's so big, Oliver. Weren't you afraid?"

"Only when I got outside and thought about it. But... not in my heart. I love you, Molly."

"Excuse me?"

"Some fights you can't lose, Molly."

"What did you say?"

"I said...some fights..."

"No! Before that!"

"Well...maybe I'll step outside."

"You have a habit of saying "Well"...Oliver. Does it mean we should pause before you move to the next baloney? Or... is it something I can dip my bucket into?"

"I said "I love you!"...drink that!"

It was quiet on the other side of the door. After a minute, she said "Well...I already knew it."

"Are you coming up?"

"Yes...I'll be up soon. Oliver...thanks for saying it."

He went outside. Then Norm and Marlaine came out, and said they were going down to the shops.

Norm said, "Oliver, are you yet in the mood for this climb?"

"Sure!"

"Do you want Bush off it?"

"No. I see no reason to put him aside."

"I've hired two porters," Norm said, shrugging his shoulders. "I was planning to wait for the Sherpa lady to bring hers, but I met a couple young men while shopping...and they were so smiley and enthusiastic, I didn't want to refuse them."

Marlaine asked "Have you seen Shoree? She's disappeared. The Sherpa lady wants her to help in the kitchen."

Oliver said "I last saw her...just before Bush and I got to fighting."

Norm said "She was watching you through the dormitory window...and went out after you and Bush finished. Maybe she walked down to the shops."

"Yeh, probably," said Oliver.

Marlaine said "The Sherpa lady hopes she hasn't run of to Thame, as she did last month...for a couple days."

CHAPTER SIX

Wanting his lighter jacket, the red and black one, Oliver went to his room. As he opened the door, he nearly stepped on a piece of white paper about the size of the hotel's menu notebook. On it were words written with a black crayon. He picked it up.

> Oliver
>   I'll come to your room at midnight. But have no candle burning.
>   I must have darkness.
>   I'm so shy.
>   I know you won't believe I wrote this,
> but I did.
>   Shoree

Oliver said, aloud, "No!...Shoree...I think you didn't."
    He knocked on Molly's door and, hearing no response, said "Molly, I'll be upstairs."

The only person in the dining room was Mr. Barton. As Oliver went to him, he lightly noted the presence of the book John Finn spoke of.

Barton seemed unaware of his arrival, so Oliver sat near him and looked through the window. He was glad he did. In this late afternoon, although darkness lay low on the mountainside beyond the river valley, the town and all else around had an outstanding goldness.

Molly appeared at the curtains. "I'm having tea. Would you like some?"

"Yes, Molly…my biscuit with jam."

Mr. Barton said "Would you please order me a cup of black tea?" He had turned in his chair to face them.

Molly asked "And a biscuit?"

"Toast…thanks."

After Molly went out, Mr. Barton looked at Oliver. "Glad to see you. I was almost certain you would win the fight."

Oliver moved closer. They shook hands.

"Because I was in the right?"

"I think that helps…but, it was because you seem to have what it takes." He smiled. "Other than that, Oliver Faulkner, your path seems to be…where there's gold on a snowy mountain. And, so…best served by winning."

Oliver put his hand on the table, and looked at the swollen, darkened, knuckles. "And Bush is best served, at this time, by losing? He was being an ass, and needed a chance to get beyond it?"

"Sure, Oliver! And so…probably…he also won. But my certainty rested on feeling. Intuition. And it's easy to be wrong. Often the touch of death can't be essayed with a clear mind. People die taking their kids to Disneyland. I'm glad you won."

Molly brought in the tea. And he saw that her black jacket and sweater matched his, but the dominant part was as before...the blond hair...some of which was loose and down to her chin.

"Molly...your hair is a bit darker today. It's closer to light brown. What happened?"

"It became true to itself. I like your black sweater, Oliver. It highlights your blue eyes."

Molly had two plates with toast, one with twice as much on it as the other.

Mr. Barton said "I'll be leaving for Tyangboche in the morning. Will I see you two again?"

"We'll be there tomorrow, right Oliver? And so...Mr. Barton...you can tell us your story."

Oliver asked "Can you do that now? Some of it?"

Mr. Barton looked through the window but, after a few seconds passed, he turned to them again. "My wife died here thirty years ago. Actually, she died above, at Lobuche, and they brought her here, hoping to revive her." He sighed. "I had gone to climb Pumo Ri...which is not so high as Everest and Lhotse and them, but dangerous because of falling debris...so I left her in Lobuche, in what I thought were safe hands. While I was gone she got altitude problems, both cerebral and pulmonary. They waited too long before bringing her down. And that's why I've been sitting here...trying to see her again. You can call me Greg."

"Did you?" asked Molly. "See her?"

"No!"

Oliver said "I was told…you have the ability to leave your body." He cleared his throat, and spoke more gently. "Is that the way you were trying to see her?"

Greg said "It seems…my central consciousness, my "I", can get a short distance away. Usually about six feet. Then I'm above, looking down at my body, and those around me. But…I might have only dreamed it."

Oliver said "I did that once. When I was thirteen. I was suddenly just there, above, looking down at my body reading aloud from a book."

Greg said "I believe we have a body-mind and a soul. But at the death of the body…only the soul goes on. The inner "I" consciousness."

Oliver said "I think most existents don't have "I", but sentience resides in all things. Pure consciousness is in every unit that maintains according to the laws. So…when the "I" of the soul goes on, it's accompanied by the form of the body that soul was in."

"Then why didn't he see his wife?" asked Molly.

Greg said "What do we know of other dimensions?

Maybe our souls need to have passed on…before we can see a soul. Or, as Oliver points out, see body and soul."

"What of ghosts?" Molly asked.

"I don't know," said Greg. "Oliver…?"

Oliver shrugged his shoulders. "Maybe your wife doesn't want to rush you."

Molly said "It would be sad that he can't see her, because she doesn't feel like coming around today. But do you think it would be sadder if she did?"

"Molly, I think it could be. Greg…do you sometimes feel her presence?"

Greg looked down at the floor. "Yeh! But I don't need to be here, in Namche...to do that. And it happens, usually, when I'm not trying to."

"She could be here now," said Oliver.

Molly said "Let's not talk about it. Greg...I hope you see your wife again...when it's time. Anyway, I believe in Heaven!" Then she added, in a gentler tone, "Eat your toast!"

Getting off the bench, she walked a few feet away, toward the kitchen. She stopped by the book Curt put on the table.

Greg Barton got up. "I'll have a nap...and a short walk. If I don't see you two tonight, I hope we meet above, in Tyangboche. Goodbye, Molly." He shook hands again with Oliver, and then departed.

CHAPTER SEVEN

Looking down at the book, Oliver said ""In The Palm of the Lotus". It's a collection of quotes...with lengthy comments about them. He pretends that the comments are his... but they're not. I know the man who put this together. He's from New Hampshire. He's rich...and on the way to being governor of that state. What he is now, among other things, is a liar and a braggart."

"How did it get here?" asked Molly.

"As my fight ended, Curt ran up the stairs...into here. In and out. John saw him...then came and found the book."

"Oliver...right where you sit?"

"Yeh...but for a moment let's put aside what we make of it. I've got to show you the note...someone put under my door."

He gave her the note.

"I'm stepping into the kitchen, Molly. When I come back we'll talk about these things."

In the kitchen the Sherpa lady and the grandmother were at the stoves, each busy peeling a potato.

"Namaste. Is Shoree in the building?"

The grandmother said "Ah!...Shoree! I love you!"

"No!" said Oliver. "I don't! I mean…I do…as a friend."

The Sherpa lady continued to peel as she spoke. "She's gone to visit."

"Tyangboche," the grandmother said.

"No! Thame!" said the Sherpa lady. "She always tells me if she goes to see her boy. But this time she said nothing. I have a sister in Thame." She sighed, then she looked at Oliver. "She'll be back soon. Maybe tonight."

He turned to go. "I'll see her then."

"You're bad!" said the grandmother, laughing afterward.

"I only want to talk with her."

The grandmother put down her knife and did her dance, walking bowlegged around the room, and trying to make her face show delight.

He tried not to laugh, but he did. "Stop!" he said. "It's you I love."

Grandmother ran to her daughter's side and hugged her, now pretending to be afraid. "He comes to me, tonight. I'll be smiling in the dark."

She commenced to peel, as before, but spoke rapidly in Nepali.

The Sherpa lady translated. "She said Shoree's husband is bad. He hits her. Also…she said "Are Nepalis not good enough for you?"

Oliver was quiet a few seconds. Then he went to stand nearer to them. "If Shoree were the girl I loved, I'd marry her."

The grandmother worked on, and didn't look up. She said "We'll make this Sherpa stew for Oliver." Then she looked at him. "For you and Shoree."

"And for Molly?"

She looked at her hands again, as she worked.

The Sherpa lady stopped peeling and stared at her mother.

The old lady said "Yes...for Molly, too."

As he entered the dining room, Molly was looking at the book. He sat beside her.

"What do you think of the note?" he asked.

She had placed it on the table, beside the book. Now she said "The candles here are the size of your little finger, and give faint light." Then she shuddered. "Whoever wrote the note...needs a darker darkness."

"Yes, Molly. Beautiful Shoree doesn't."

"How do you know?" she asked.

"I can see through her clothes. I mean...the same way you can. Of course...I don't. I did. Last year I wondered about it."

She laughed. "So what's the connection to the book? Obviously, you're making one. Did Curt leave this book for you to find? Did he write the note?"

Oliver picked up the book. "This man, Elmer Wallace, is wealthy...and has power through selling land to the state of New Hampshire. Everyone knows he wants to be governor."

"Did you insult his book?"

"Yes...at a party...when I could no longer bear to listen to his bragging. But...that's not why I made a connection. One day I went to a friend's house...in New Hampshire... and Elmer Wallace was there, and my friend's thirteen year old daughter. He was doing it to her. So, I kicked him out. Grabbed him by the collar and tossed him. I told him if he went there again, I'd tell my friend what happened."

"But you didn't tell your friend?"

"I did…a week later. After it happened, I was told she's fifteen…and promiscuous. When I caught them she was on top. So…I hesitated."

"It's wrong, Oliver…and he could have had serious trouble."

"That might be the connection, Molly. Mainly that he could lose his political future. But…why would Curt bring this book to me? Nah! It doesn't seem likely. Also, why would he write a note, pretending he's Shoree?"

"Oliver, we're having strong feelings. We both know there might be no connection…but it's too dark in this area of coincidence, to let Curt be free of being tied to it. When I first met him, in Lukla, we sat together at dinner…without rapport…and without any apparent desire to overcome lack of interest in one another…we only sat and ate. Then… coldly, he put his hand on my shoulder and said "Your room or mine?"

"Molly, he's an ass! But it could be that Shoree wrote the note. And maybe Curt found this book in Connecticut and, while he was rushing, after my fight, absent-mindedly dropped it here, where I sit. Ah!…let's put it out of our heads. Tonight I'll lock my door…and not give a damn who comes to it."

He picked up the book. "Perhaps…Curt is wanting to lighten his mind. These quotes are from great minds. The words were shifted by Wallace, but the meaning in them is the same. I…"

That's when a piece of white paper, with writing on it, fell from the book to the table. Large words were printed on it. Oliver read them, aloud.

I know of a girl about fourteen
who is pregnant. Now you know it.

CHAPTER EIGHT

At dinnertime, candlelight danced on the windows. A burst of hail struck the glass. Molly wore her dark blue parka again, and the red turtleneck. And Oliver thought she seemed physically smaller, and more in need of being cared for...so, as they sat on the bench, he put his arm around her shoulders, and pulled her in.

She looked up at him, then rested her head against his chest, where his parka was unzipped.

"You and I never did fight yet," she said.

"Yes...we did. Remember about the cloned sheep?"

"Will you take a shower, Oliver?"

"Why? Do I smell ready for one?"

"Yes!"

"You, too!" He put his face into the hair at the top of her head. "Your hair reminds me of a bird's nest."

"Excuse me...?"

"It's so comfy and warm. I'll take a shower in Tyangboche. If you wait, we can do it together…in a dark, tin-lined room under the kitchen. Well…it has one hanging light bulb."

"That sounds romantic, Oliver…bathing together in a dungeon. But I'll wait 'til then."

Everyone came to the tables except Greg Barton and Curt.

When the Sherpa lady came in he asked about Shoree, and she motioned with her hand toward the northwest. "Yes, she went to Thame. They saw her on the trail."

In awhile the Sherpa lady brought glowing embers to the pot-bellied stove at the center of the dining room. She put a few leather-topped stools near it, and John Finn went there to sit.

Oliver asked…"John, will you walk down tomorrow, to Lukla?"

Marlaine cut in. "Mr. Finn…tomorrow they have the bazaar. You should stay to see it."

"Did they call you Huckleberry?" asked Bush, whose face was swollen and darkly colored around the eyes. And when Norm punched him on the shoulder, he said "But I was trying to be friendly." He looked directly at John. "I like you."

"I wasn't called that," John said. "But I was a free spirit. Pretty much on my own." He raised his shoulders. "My mother was always working. Well, those were tough times, the twenties and thirties."

Norm asked "But you got through school?"

"Yeh…in my own way. My main teacher was the Columbia River. I've been a fisherman all my life. But I did lots of other things."

"World War Two," said Oliver.

"I was a tail gunner on B-25s…in the Pacific."
Bush asked "Did you work on the Alaska pipeline?"
"Yeh…I did that."

John got up and, with his cup of tea, came to sit at Oliver's right side. "I'm hungry," he said. "I've done enough talkin'." He scrunched himself way down in his parka, slapped one hand onto the table, and with the other picked up his cup and sipped from it.

Oliver lifted his own cup.

That's when Molly's hand reached in front of him to John's hand, the one flat on the table. She held it about ten seconds.

John had some color in his cheek. "Thanks! If Oliver doesn't bring you home with him, I won't let him off the plane."

Porters came in and went to a table at the wall away from the windows. There were five young men. Norm said three were his, for him and Bush and Marlaine, and that he hired them for three days. "To Lobuche. Then they can wait until the return from above. But I might decide to use them all the way." He added "The other two men are wanting to porter for you and Molly."

"If you use them above Lobuche," said Oliver, "You'll need to provide a tent, and trail food, and warm sleeping bags. And maybe an item or two of clothing."

Oliver spoke to Molly. "I'll hire a porter for two days. To Pheriche only…and not to wait for me there, but to return here. Twenty dollars is appropriate for that time and distance. If you agree to do the same, they can carry half our loads. That'll give us a couple days of moderate conditioning."

"No. I'll go to them." He looked at Molly. "This is to avoid an unintentional rudeness developing in young porters. They try to insult you into hiring them. With a laugh… they'll say you're incapable, for this reason or that, of carrying your own load."

"They look so innocent…and smiley."

"They are!"

He went to them and stood near their table.

"Namaste. Are you wanting to porter for me and my wife?"

One of them pointed to young men at the end of the bench. Those two jumped up.

"Yes! We go with you to Lobuche, and wait for you."

"No!" said Oliver. "To Pheriche. Two days work…but I'll pay you for four. And you return alone from there. We don't need you to wait. Twenty two dollars each."

"You can't do it!" said the young man, waving a hand before him, as though to erase Oliver's beliefs.

"You're not used to it. And your wife is not strong enough. I can tell."

Oliver moved two steps toward his own table, then turned to the young man. "Then I'll hire someone else."

"No! You hire us!" the young man assured him. "But that blond man, with Shoree, would pay much more, He said!"

"Twenty two," said Oliver.

"All right!" the porter agreed. "But you should get plenty of rest tonight. We leave at eight…and walk an hour before the sun is bright."

"I leave, usually, at seven thirty," said Oliver. "If you want the job be here by then."

When he got to his table, he told Molly about the deal; also, about one of them having seen Curt with Shoree.

He told John Finn that he ordered hot water for a shower, but decided to wait another day, so the water would be available for him if he wanted it.

After eating, he and Molly went into the kitchen, and stood near the curtains.

"Excuse me!" he said to the Sherpa lady. "What time do you bar the door?"

"When it gets dark," she said. "If everyone is in."

"And so…you're waiting for Shoree?"

"No. Shoree is not coming, tonight. The door is barred. My mother just did it."

"You're not waiting for Curt?"

She looked down at the large basin she was near, as she washed dishes. "Curt is not coming. My friend saw him walking on the Thame trail…with Shoree."

CHAPTER NINE

They were moving down the dark stairs, and Molly was holding his arm.

"It always scares me," she said, "To be in such darkness, where your life has you expecting at least a tiny bit of light."

Pulling out his flashlight, he directed the beam to the steps. Then he stopped walking, and aimed it farther below, at the outer door.

He laughed. "There's the two by four John could have used."

"What for?"

"He said that during the fight he was about to leap out the window and help me."

"Oliver, we didn't say goodbye to him."

"We can in the morning. He gets up early."

He shined his light into the dormitory, and moved a step toward it.

"Don't!" Molly said, gripping his arm more firmly. "It's too dark...and no one ever goes in there." She shivered. "Leave it alone!"

They went down their hallway, stopping at her door.

He asked "Which room is Curt's?"

"The one beside yours. We passed it. It's locked."

"Beside mine...? And yet...when I was fighting, he was in my room." He paused, and sighed. "But, so was John. They both were. Ah...it's nothing! Let's forget Curt. He's gone!"

Molly held open her door. "Will you shine your light here, Oliver? Please come in...and stay until I get my candles burning."

They went in.

"If you have two, light 'em both. Put one on the window counter and the other on the table. Molly, pack everything tonight. I'll knock on your door at six."

When the candles were lit he put the flashlight away.

Her sleeping bag was laid out on a bunk. He touched it, and asked "Is this bag warm?"

The bunks were nearly three feet high, and she now stood there, feeling the bag. Without answering, she turned to face him and, with her butt against the bed, folded her arms and unfolded them, and cleared her throat. She held onto the edge of the bed, and looked at his chest.

"Oliver...I believe you. I think...we'll be together a while. And that's a long time."

"Yes, Molly. You mean when I said I love you? Well, I do."

"I'm so glad," she said.

He stepped toward her.

"Stop!" she was holding up her hand between them. "I feel it would be right for us to sleep together tonight."

"Shall we?" he asked.

"No!" she said. "But it seems like a mistake for us not to. Why should you be over there...and me over here?"

"And so...?" he wondered.

"So...Oliver, I hate to say goodnight."

He waited. But she didn't say any more.

"Molly...what's the final word?"

She said "I love you, too. Get out!"

In his room, he repacked his gear, leaving out towel and soap, toothbrush and paste. As he was doing that he remembered about the basin of water he had planned to bring down, so he blew out the candles and went into the hall again.

Curt's door was locked.

Before climbing the stairs, he remembered Molly saying the dormitory's darkness seemed to be darker because of the feeling of a constant emptiness...and this made him begin to dismiss his unease. After he got water from the kitchen and came back down he was not so aware of that room.

Again he shined the light on the outer door. It was barred, and the angle of the two by four was the same as earlier. It was about a half inch lower on one end.

He reentered his room and lit a candle. All he did with the water was wash his face and hands, aware now that by the next day's end a black dust would cover his body. So he wondered why he didn't think of it earlier and save himself a walk up the stairs. He could have washed lightly in the morning.

He lay on his bag and looked at the ceiling. It had separated slats, but he knew the dining room floor was just there. But during his seven years of visiting Nepal he had been under many ceilings with no floor above, only a dark room, or the sky. And sometimes he saw the moon and stars.

He had been in places with no lock on the door, and some with no door. But he had always felt safe. One night in Nuntala a cat-like creature, except that it was long and had a bushy tail, leaped through the window to his floor and went under the door into the hallway.

He sat up and, looking at his door, saw that the base of this one was only about an inch above the floor.

With clothes on, he blew out his candle and slipped into the bag. Then he noticed light shining through the wall, to his left. It went out. Which reminded him of the nature of these buildings, that they also often had spaces between wall boards. So he didn't think any more about it.

He was sleepy...and began to drift away.

Immediately he entered a scary dream, one he recognized...and woke up. It was of an event from years earlier, and he had dreamed of it several times, in the past. And now he had the emotion of it again.

He and a friend were driving a car at night, through a California redwood forest...and decided to stop at the road's edge, and sleep. So, he was in the front seat and the other man in the back. A car passed, then another. And suddenly he had a sense of danger. That's when his friend shouted "Let's get out of here!"

Oliver sat up in his bag, now, yet remembering...yet feeling...what he later called "The seeming approach of death".

He saw that it was midnight, as he flashed a match near his watch. He got out of bed and, putting on his boots, and dropping the flashlight into his pants pocket, slowly moved to the door and stood beside it, in the corner of the room toward Curt's...where he could feel the door, and the cracks in the wall.

The door moved. The back of his right hand felt it. Putting the fingers of his left hand there he yet was aware of pressure being applied from the other side, heavily. He could feel it and hear it, as the wood fibers moved. And now the metal parts did...in a clicking sound at the bolt.

Oliver went to his window sill and lit both candles. Grabbing his stick, he went to the door, smashed the bolt aside with his fist, and waited.

Nothing happened.

He stepped into the hallway, quickly flashing light in both directions. There was no one to be seen. So he walked to his left to the end of the hall, to the empty room, and opened its door and looked within. It was empty.

The door to the room next to his, at that end, opened, and John Finn came out.

"You scared the crap out of me!" he yelled. "I thought I was on a boat and a sealion was coming in after my fish... and he thought I was one."

"Sorry, John!...you must have heard me slam the door bolt. Let me get past you! Someone was trying to get into my room."

Molly appeared, shining her light on them, and on Curt's locked door.

They all directed light to the dormitory entrance. Then Oliver went to where he could see both up the stairs and to the outer door, below, and he saw that the two by four was resting, upright, against the wall.

He went down and put it into the holders, so it was once again a barrier.

CHAPTER TEN

Oliver and Molly walked northward beside the Dudh Kosi, below and to the right. There were fewer trees now, but the way was comfortably pleasant with the sky blue and the mountains bright. You could see Lhotse…just before Everest. But…here…the dominant aspect was of Ama Dablam. It was across the river, ahead.

Molly said "The blue is not so deep as at evening. Now the hills…although brightly lit, are not so golden. But…"

"I'm so glad for your "but", Molly."

"Such beauty!" she said. "I can hardly stand it!"

She had stopped walking and stood looking with her mouth wide open.

He grabbed her and, after she was looking entirely into his eyes, kissed her.

"The sun's getting up," he said. "Let's stop in this little place." He pointed to the only building. It showed as one-room, to the left of the trail and slightly above it. A table was on the porch. "I remember this. There's a couple tables inside. You can sit in the shade and look down to the river."

The building's front had a two-feet high barrier, with an opening in the center. They rested their packs against that little wall, and went in and sat at one of the tables.

He held her hand.

Molly whispered "They live in the back. Look at the closets…with the glass doors…and the dark wood of it, so cared for. We can buy biscuits here."

"She does," he said. "She lives in the back. With a tot." Then he looked out. "When we get down to the river and cross, we won't see her again."

"Who?" asked Molly.

"The river. She goes northwest…up to Gokyo."

Molly looked out. "I can see a river coming past Ama Dablam…up toward Everest."

"That's the Imja Khola. We'll be walking beside it."

"It?" So…you have a special feeling for "her". She pointed downward. "When we cross this river…will you say "Goodbye, Miss Dudh…I love you"!…?

"I might! She goes by other names, some centuries old. Imja Drangpa, for one. I've watched her dance, edge to edge, only a dozen times…but that's enough time to make "it" stick in my throat."

"Not because of familiarity," said Molly. "There are other rivers you know well, you wouldn't laugh and cry for."

"Yeh…a feeling pops in and sings a song."

He put his hand on the back of her neck, and moved his fingers into her hair. "I love you…my biscuit with jam on it."

Molly said "That's what you meant in Namche! I told the lady you wanted tea…and your biscuit. I wondered why she laughed."

The Nepali lady came out. She had two children with her, one about three, the other a year old and crawling.

"Namaste"…he said to her. "Dui cup chiyaa, dinos. Ahh… lemon tea."

The girl smiled and bowed. She turned away, taking two steps toward the gallon-size thermos on the shelf at the glass cupboard. Then she stopped, bent over, and with hands to her mouth, seemed to be shaking…to be trembling.

The girl stood up and smiled. "I remember you!"

She went to the cupboards and poured tea.

Molly said "What is it she remembers?"

"Esko mol kati ho?" he asked of the girl, pointing to a jar of candy kisses.

"All of them?" the girl said, wide-eyed.

"No! Ten."

The girl said "Duitaa tin mol. Two for one a half rupee."

"I'll have ten, please."

After she brought the tea and candy, Oliver said "Dhanyabad. Do I speak Nepali…" he was searching for a word, but he didn't know whether to say "good" or "bad".

"No!" the girl answered, smiling. Then she turned and went into the back room.

Molly said "It's OK, Oliver…there are times blushing shows humility." She slid her chair next to his.

"Molly…I broke rungs in my ladder. I did it."

She leaned against him. "But you're not at the bottom of it, Oliver. Kiss me!" She pointed to her lips. "Here!…where you're at the top."

He kissed her.

He said "Our lips go together." But when she laughed at that, he added "Many lips don't. Except for you and…I would have gone through life thinking kissing was good but not great."

"And who…?" she asked. "Me and who?"

"Nobody! A pair of lips."

She said "This place was once under the sea."

"What does that have to do with lips?"

"I could make mine hard, Oliver. You might say you saw me in the mountains. What was her name?"

"Who?"

"Me!" she said. "I better be more than a pair of lips."

The girl came in.

Molly said, shyly, and with a smile, "Biscoot, dinos!"

The girl opened the cupboard and showed Molly several kinds of plastic-wrapped cookies, each pack about five inches long, manufactured in Kathmandu or India. She asked for the coconut flavor, and held up two fingers. "Dui. Thanks. Dhanyabad."

They paid the bill and went outside.

"There's my sister and the others," she said, looking south.

As they faced that way the trail was up, gently, a hundred yards, before disappearing west. The others had just come around the hill.

Oliver put on his pack. to wait."

"We'll lose time, Molly…and walk that much longer, in greater heat than this. Before getting to Tyangboche we'll need to climb almost straight up. Is Greg Barton with them?"

"Yes…he's well ahead. In all Nepal only Greg Barton has a walking stick like yours. There you are…in thirty years."

"Thanks. I feel complimented. But..."

"Oliver...he's handsome and thoughtful-looking. And see how easily he leads the others. I'm sure he isn't trying to, but he is. Even if he were behind...he would be. Why did you say "But...?"

"Because he's alone."

She said "I didn't mean that...you know I didn't."

"He kissed her, then hugged her.

The others arrived and went immediately in for tea, except that Marlaine called Molly aside.

Oliver went in.

Norm said "What happened last night? I heard a loud noise, then you and John Finn were talking."

Bush said "I thought you were chasing a rat. Then I thought "No!...I must be dreaming."

Molly and Marlaine came in.

Oliver described the note which was put under his door, and told them of the book and the reference to the pregnant girl, and about the man in New Hampshire.

"Slow down!" Bush said. "Shoree sent you the note, but she didn't come back?"

"Curt sent it!" Said Norm. "Most likely."

Marlaine said "And both of them are gone."

"I'm worried about Shoree," said Oliver. "Before we departed I told the Sherpa lady about my concern."

Marlaine spoke to Oliver. "Curt has gone to Khumjung. After you and Molly left, someone came in from there. He told the lady he saw Curt going that way...from the northeast corner of Namche."

"Khumjung is the town above the reforestation patch," said Molly. "Why would he head for Thame, then slip back above us?"

Oliver answered. "If slip is the right word…you can go to Khumjung, and then rejoin this trail above, before you get to Tyangboche." He pointed his thumb upward. "The trail is above us."

Molly said "He could roll rocks onto us?"

"No! If you went up this hill and down the other side to a stream, and crossed it, you'd find that trail. He's probably on it."

He asked Greg Barton how he was feeling.

"I'm fine. It's nine o'clock, Oliver…and Molly…so I'll be on your heels another hour." He smiled. "Don't do anything romantic."

"But…we might…just around the bend," she said.

After he and Molly got walking again, and were a couple hundred feet downward toward the river, a helicopter arrived from the south. It hovered a moment before the little building, then came along to them, the whole craft rotating once, fully, before continuing north.

"That was John Finn!" said Oliver.

Molly sighed. "Remember…Marlaine just took me aside? I forgot to tell you what she had to say. Maybe on purpose. Oliver, she took this from Curt's room." She felt around in her jacket pocket…then handed him a roll of money. "It's twenty five, hundred dollar bills. And this picture of you was in his wallet, in a secret compartment."

He put the money and picture into a zippered pocket inside his jacket.

"Also…" Molly went on, "She stole this…from John Finn. Three thousand dollars."

She handed him that, as well.

"That explains the helicopter," he said. "You told the sherpa lady about Marlaine's stealing…and so, John knows where to look."

They descended to the river, and walked onto the low bridge, an arc-shaped wooden one made of hewed lumber, some of the pieces loose in the walkway of it. Two cables ran at shoulder height, and a pile of white boulders were under the wood at the ends.

They were on it when the helicopter came back down the valley. The craft passed no more than thirty feet above them, and the pilot was sitting alone in it.

CHAPTER ELEVEN

It was just after noon when they finished the steep climb to Tyangboche. The trail had passed through a pine forest, but was mostly unshaded. And now, as they came to the level, they rested.

Molly pulled up her pants to the knees, showing her legs with fine, black dust.

He reached down and touched her. "Some of this comes from India."

She said "How can it be so hot, here, at thirteen thousand feet?"

"Let's go, Molly! We'll get tea...and have a talk with John. Then we'll ask about a hot shower...for later."

Leaving low pines, they stepped into an open area which sloped gently downward several hundred yards toward the north. Centered were a couple one-story buildings, and immediately to the left, just above this level, was the monastery. At the foot of that was a teahouse.

He said "At this edge of the hill, in the trees beside the monastery...is the hotel I like. There's John." He pointed. "See those tables outside the teahouse?"

They walked slowly toward John...then waved at him.

Oliver, I think John is mad at us. Or else...he's sleeping with his eyes open."

When they got to him he smiled weakly.

They sat and ordered tea.

Oliver told the girl "And a Fanta orange soda. Thanks." And after she turned away, to take Molly's order, "Hello, John."

"Howdy." John said, without expression, and looking to the edge of the hill, at the trailside they came from.

"We have your money." He put it on the table. "Just before you passed in the helicopter, Marlaine told Molly about it...and gave it to her."

John glanced at it.

"So...the pilot couldn't wait for you, John? He had another job, and needed to rush away. Is that it?"

"Yeh. My head feels really big."

"Had anything to eat?"

"Nah. I'm not hungry."

Oliver looked at Molly, and whispered. "That's another sign of trouble. He doesn't eat breakfast...so he ought to be hungry by now." Again he spoke to John, as he touched his shoulder. "I need to see how strong you are. Please walk with me to this other table."

John looked at the ground and his own tea cup, and again at Oliver. When Oliver motioned with his hand for him to get up, he did. Then slowly, but with apparent steadiness, he began to walk beside Oliver toward the table. On the way his foot came down upon the edge of a raised rock, one that was a few inches higher than the others and prominently there, causing him to stumble badly.

Oliver helped him return to the table. "I'm taking you down...to the bottom of the hill. Wait here until I get a room for Molly and me."

They went to the hotel in the pines and registered at a counter just inside the door. A tall, thin sherpani of midage, wearing an apron over a woolen dress with no sleeves, and a white sweater under that, took them to the second floor, and to a room looking south, through the upper part of the trees. She presented a notebook and had them write what they wanted for supper. And they asked about hot water for a shower.

She said two of the pages in the notebook belonged to them. She smiled, and departed.

In the room, Oliver dropped his pack onto the bunk to the left, and expected Molly to put hers on the other. She didn't. She put it beside his.

"But...they are narrow, aren't they," she said, moving her pack to the other bunk. "Shall we see what's around the bend?"

Looking at his watch, he said "Molly, I'll try to be here before dark. Keep your door locked...until Marlaine and Greg Barton arrive. I'll tell them where you are. Dammit!"

"What, Oliver?"

"We're beginning to live Curt's life...and that nitwit in New Hampshire, the would-be governor."

She said "Do you think he was paid that...to kill you?" She touched his pocket where he had the money.

"Yes...it seems likely."

"But, Oliver, did you see where I first put my pack?"

She stepped to him...until their bodies touched.

"Yes, Molly...and my heart raced."

"Oliver, I think things work out...the way fate intends."

"Maybe she knows I'll be careful to bring my heart back to you. On the carpet...freewill gets the parties to the right place for the seers eyes. But...maybe destiny is smiling, too."

"Then, Oliver...the lady is a valid part of reality?"

"I wish I knew. Anyway...next time I'm between thoughts...ask me then, Molly."

He departed...and, after returning to John, led him to the edge of the hill.

"How do you feel?"

"Seventy five...and out of water."

"Get on my back!" said Oliver. He turned his body.

Without a word, John got on.

After about a dozen steps, Oliver said "That's how I know you're sick. Yesterday, you would have kicked me when I bent over...and told me to get in the lifeboat."

"Will you fall?"

"No!"

"Well...I already knew that."

After a half hour of sweating and straining...near the bottom of the hill he met the others.

"You must be strong," yelled Marlaine. "How can you carry that much? John...are you all right?"

"Yes...I think I can walk now."

Oliver said "Bush...it's about five hundred feet to that huge boulder with the ancient carvings on it. We'll be at the bottom then, where he can walk more easily. Will you carry him to it?"

Norm and Greg helped John to the ground and onto Bush's back. So, Bush brought John down to the boulder.

"Thanks, kid" Then the old man held forward his hand.

"Anytime, young feller." Bush smiled, showing that he had a couple teeth missing on his jaw's left side. "How old are you? Oh…I remember."

"Thirty eight…or thereabouts. Now get your butt up the hill, before it gets dark."

As Bush was disappearing, John said, lowly, "Curt was seen in Khumjung. Did you know he can rejoin this trail above Tyangboshe?"

"Yes. Also, he can rejoin it here," said Oliver, pointing to a trail coming in from the west. But that's enough about him. I don't want to live his life."

John snorted. "If he comes screaming at you with a knife…you'll have to live his life."

Oliver said "But he isn't doing that now. Look, John! That small building ahead is what I planned to bring you to. You can spend the night. She has a boy about seven, and he carved this knife for me."

Reaching into his pocket, he took out a piece of wood and handed it over.

"You carried this from Alaska…just to show the boy?"

"Yes. I thought I would see him, when Molly and I passed earlier. He was at school. So, will you show it to him? I'll get if from you in Alaska. And…maybe you can give him this." He brought out a small, folding knife.

John took the knives. "Oliver, you better get going. That hill is a killer. It'll be dark soon." He kicked the ground, then looked down at it and said "Sorry!"

"John…did you apologize to me, or to the earth?"

"I saw a man do that just the other day. A skinny, Nepali man…who lives on the other side of the world from me. But it reminded me how we're all the same, in what we ought to cherish. In the beginning we are. Then we drift away."

"I've got to get moving!"

"Yes!" said John. "Hurry to the forest! The late hours are best…for death by ambush."

"John…I have to go! Molly will need me! And you just told me you think it's time."

"I know! You ought to climb it now. I'm tellin' ya to be careful."

They shook hands and hugged each other, briefly.

Oliver said, "In the last ten years I only hugged two men, and both are the same size. You and Sanu, who sells an instrument called a gaini."

He turned away.

At the base of the hill he acknowledged twilight, then moved quickly and easily through it…up to where he met Bush and the others, earlier. He saw an article of clothing fifty feet ahead, tied to a tree branch, and figured it must have been attached by one of his friends. A turn in the trail was there and, so, perhaps they wanted to guide him.

He went to it and found a wool scarf of a light grey color. It was recently made, he decided, and well made…to be warm and comfortable. He wondered why anyone would part with it.

It had blood on it. Suddenly…because of that…he made a connection, remembering having seen it before.

There was a big pine to his left, at the edge of the trail. He went to it and leaned his back against it, looking carefully ahead. The darkness lay in many places.

It was Shoree's scarf. She wore it by the archway, that first time they renewed friendship. He folded the scarf and put it into his pocket.

Moving upward, he held forward the flashlight, but didn't turn it on. And at the dark places he readied himself to fight, expecting to be attacked, realizing the advantage would be with the one waiting.

Soon it was all darkness, and he would flash light, to see a length of trail.

His head told him he likely would be attacked, but there was no feeling that told him death was "right there"...ready to touch him.

He was getting near to the top of the hill, and the moon was coming up, making it easier to move. Aware that he had often found danger at the very end of climbs, there where you think it's over and you're safe, he retained his carefulness. But he wasn't feeling a threat. His thoughts went to Molly, and her safety, and that of his other friends.

He made his way to the hotel.

In the dining room, at its center, he found Molly and the others huddled around a wood stove...in the dim light... their place ringed by candled tables.

Molly hugged him. "I didn't think you'd come...it's so dark out! How is John?"

"He was recovering. I left him at a safe place."

"You should eat! I ordered a shower, Oliver. They pour the water down a pipe into the basement...as you know." She looked around the room. "Don't you think it's romantic, the way the shadows are dancing on the walls?"

Marlaine said "Tell him, Molly!"

"I will. It's bad news, Oliver. I..."

Oliver didn't press her for it, believing he knew what it was.

A Nepali girl of about thirteen came in and he ordered Dal Bhaat, and hot chocolate and tea, and asked her to bring the tea first.

"Oliver...Shoree is dead. She was strangled." Molly sighed." Just after you left to help John get down the hill, a Nepali trader came through and told the people at the monastery. We saw her little boy. Tomorrow he's to go down to Namche to be with his mother. I mean...with his grandmother."

He showed the scarf. "On the way back up...I found this on the trail, hanging from a branch. I remember Shoree wearing it. And there's blood on it."

"Ahh!...poor Shoree," said Molly. "And her mother, and the little boy."

"He was watching us?" Marlaine said.

The young girl brought tea.

"Thanks for the tea," he said. "Ask your mother to hang a lantern...please...if she has kerosene. If she's short of it... it's OK, the candles will do." He put his arm around Molly.

Norm said "We asked her to burn candles...to honor Shoree." He put his arm around Marlaine, which act seemed to purposely follow Oliver's. "We like it this way."

"Suit yourself," said Oliver. "It does reflect a trembling condition. Now I'm looking there..." He pointed. "Where candlelight is moving obtrusively on the glass, the source being near to it."

"A murderer is near," said Norm. "I'm trembling, but what are you going to do about it?"

Oliver said "In Namche I opened a door for him, but he didn't enter. On the way up the hill, tonight, he could have killed me, there in the dark. So...his mindset is a mystery to me, and maybe to him."

"We need to know our own," said Greg Barton.

"Lock your doors tonight," Oliver said. "Tomorrow I'll walk alone. "No!...with Molly. She's part of me, and a likely target...so I'll have her near."

Greg Barton said "But we should all stay near you. At least to Lobuche. We're part of you, too, Oliver...as Shoree was."

Molly asked "Lobuche...? What's there...that it would be different?"

"Sixteen thousand feet, Molly," said Oliver.

She said "And a person would be insane to go that high, or higher...to murder?"

Marlaine shuddered. "Stop it, Molly! It isn't funny!"

"Sorry! The word "insane" just slipped out."

The girl brought his Dal Bhaat, and the amount of rice could have fed the entire group, seemingly, although on one plate.

Oliver said "Thanks for honoring Shoree, with the candles."

Greg Barton said "Sorry your friend is dead, Oliver. I think you feel as I do...that she is either sleeping or her soul has gone on. And yet...in your closeness to her, your sorrow is not put away by thought."

"Sure..." Oliver agreed.

Gently, the older man said "If Shoree went on, she knows...now...winter is a sweet sadness."

Molly said "As your wife does?"

Marlaine said "Oliver, who is Curt? Why does he want to kill you?"

Briefly he retold the story. Then he said "Surely, he was paid to erase me, but let's not dwell on it. We only need to be careful."

Norm snorted "But…I want to know more about this!"

After a minute of silence, Molly said "I think Curt doesn't care about the money."

Greg Barton said "Which makes you wonder what he does care about."

"He has no compassion!" said Marlaine. "He's torturing you, and he killed Shoree…as part of it."

Oliver said "The nature of this man is yet hidden. It could be that he feels nothing…or, at times, too much."

"I saw these words of a murderer," said Norm…"I don't feel anything…I just think it's interesting to see what happens when I put the gun barrel to a head. I like to watch it blow apart"."

Greg Barton said "Such a man as the one you described, wouldn't love enough to hate much, and would feel no need to go higher than Lobuche."

Bush said "I saw a movie, once, about Ghengis Khan. It was junk. But in a book I read, it said that when he killed a neighbor he would sleep with the dead man's wife, and destroy his crops and everything else he owned."

"So…in such a case…something is missing?" said Marlaine. "Can such a man truly love anyone?"

Greg Barton said "We ought not to guess about Curt. We don't know his life. Probably we could cut through ages of it by getting to his beginnings...and assume the presence of love, there, and the destruction of it."

Oliver said "Marlaine wondered about there being something missing...making it so a person can't love in return. I...think you don't have love destroyed, only buried. And you can forget what it is, on purpose, it being something you think you can't get."

"Probably near the beginning of life," said Molly.

Oliver said "What do we know!" He sighed. "But...at the beginning we have no knowledge of life. We have proper integrity...within innocence...and feelings...but if we're hurt, can we understand it well enough to ever escape the cloud?"

"Do you care?" asked Norm. "Will you ask him while he's cutting your throat?"

Marlaine said "He ought to try understanding the man who wants to kill him!"

"While he's killing you?" Norm was grinning.

"Of course not!" said Marlaine. She got up and went to the pot-bellied stove, a couple feet away.

"Let's not talk about it!" said Oliver.

Greg Barton said "Sorry, Oliver...I know you didn't want to dwell on Curt. Talking can make things worse...it can bring contention, and raise emotion. But also it can make you feel protected somewhat. It's trying to build a wall between you and evil. I have to agree, though...we are just guessing."

Marlaine sat again.

Norm said "Curt is crazy...is what he is!"

"Shoree was beautiful," said Bush. "I had a girl." He cleared his throat, and looked away from everyone, then at the floor. "Not really! She never gave a damn about me. I took her out a couple times, is all."

Oliver saw Norm dig his elbow into Marlaine's side, and grin...in reference to Bush's words.

"You haven't taken out the right one, Bush" said Oliver. "You will...don't worry about it!"

Marlaine said, angrily, "I could love you, Bush. I don't, but I could. I think you're worth caring about."

Molly said "Mr. Barton, when did your wife die?"

"Thirty years ago. I was thirty five and she was twenty nine."

"Why are you here?" she asked. "After Namche, you wanted to do some climbing?"

Oliver said "Come with us to Changri Pass. It's beyond Gorak Shep, and west of Kala Patar. The others might want to go farther than that...but you could go that far."

Barton said "I thought about turning my nose east, at Kala Patar. But...are you familiar with Lho La, the pass into Tibet? It overlooks Everest base camp. You know of it, Oliver. Of course...you'll go to Changri La." He pronounced the ch as sh.

They all looked at Oliver.

Molly said "Shangrila...?"

"La means pass," he answered. "It's just a name. You can make of it whatever you want."

Norm said "It's in western Nepal. You walk through a dark cave, and have a spiritual experience. When you come out the end you're in Shangrila. Some monatery has ancient writings from Tibet, telling of a place you go through to a hidden valley."

Oliver got up. "Are you coming, Molly?"

She went to the kitchen door, which was heavily curtained, and the lady told her the shower was almost ready. She said there was enough hot water for two.

CHAPTER TWELVE

In their room they found soap and flashlights.
"I have an extra towel," she said, and tossed it to him. "How embarrassing...that they all know we're taking a shower together. What do they think?"

"That we met in the night and bumped." He laughed. "If we wash...we can meet in the day."

He put his arms around her. "How long do you want me to hold you?"

"Forever!"

"Then...you ought to hold me, too."

She did.

There was a knock on the door, and a strong, female voice said "You two should go down for your shower...before the water cools!"

When they left the building, and were yet near the door...in darkness...they heard the lady lock it. Her voice came through the wood, as though far away, telling them to knock very hard when ready to come back.

Molly whispered "Follow me, closely. We just need to go around to the back. Keep your stick ready!...but hold my hand!...shine your flashlight!"

"No. I can see without it. You follow me! And be quiet!"

They went down the hill about ten feet, then toward the middle of the rear of the building. Before getting to it, the smell of cattle became strong.

He touched the building's wall. They let some of the work animals sleep here. Maybe all of them, if they're in danger of being devoured."

"By what? Snow leopards?"

"Yeh. Or bears," he said. "Yettis...or..."

"Or what, Oliver?"

"The darkness in Nepal always has something in it to lock your doors against. So...they put out dogs. I haven't heard any. Maybe they're already dead." He pinched her butt.

"Why are you trying to scare me? I can imagine a hand coming at my throat."

"Molly, let go of my arm! If you hold me...and big lips wrap around your nose...how could I help you?"

She pressed her face against his side.

At the shower room entrance Molly shined the light inside.

"You go in first," she said. "Look! The shower is straight back. Use your light! Be certain there's nothing there."

"Sure! But remember to get your butt in...or big teeth will get it."

Inside, they locked the door, barring it with a two by four, then went to the back, to an area where the floor and walls were cemented.

"Who carried cement way up here?"

"Skinny legs did," he said.

"When you're ready, Oliver, we tap that pipe. Then we need to stand under it until the water is gone. The lady said. But how can we do that unless we take the shower together? But…I'm not ready to. Tomorrow maybe. If we're properly united."

"In bed…?"

"When it's the only thing we have to do. Now…we bathe. We'll make love when we can look into each other's eyes. When it's like getting married."

"I can see your eyes in the dark, Molly. You can't see mine?"

"I can! But let's not take the first time lightly. Here's a stool we can put our clothes on, after we turn out the flashlights."

"There's a valve on the pipe," he said, reaching up and opening it. A bit of water came out before he closed it. "Molly, after we turn out the lights, we'll get undressed, then tap the pipe. You can stand under it first. But as soon as you're done soaping yourself, step away so I can get under. We'll just go back and forth."

"Oliver, they call it "lather". After I lather myself. But it's OK…you can say "soaping". Although…it does sound a bit ignorant. It's just that…if we're together forever…don't talk to me like I'm a man."

"You can lather yourself, Molly. I'll soap down." He laughed. "I never said that before…soap down…and maybe never again. I might say what I please when I wash."

"We can hang our clothes on those nails…above the stool," she said.

She shut off her light and put it on the stool.

Placing his stick so that it was against the wall and touching the stool, he then turned off his light and put it beside hers.

"I wonder how much water there'll be?" he said.

"At least ten gallons, Oliver. I hope."

"There's only four nails," he said. "Put your jacket and what you're wearing above the waist…on the outside nail, to the right…and the rest on the inner nail, next to it."

He took off his boots and pants.

"I'm putting my boots to the left of the stool." Then he took off his shirt and underclothes. "Molly, our filthy clothes are touching. Are you naked?"

He reached for her, finding her shoulder.

She said "Are you wondering where I am in relation to the pipe?"

He grasped both her shoulders.

There was a loud banging on the wall, followed by the sound of cattle bellowing.

"Oliver, it's cold, and I can't see you. I could smell the yaks going by when you were fighting, in Namche. I…don't know what to do now?"

"I just want a kiss."

He stepped on a small rock; and because it dug into the arch of his foot as he was leaning that way, it took some time to get off. "I…I…I…"

"That means you're lying, Oliver. I'll remember. When you stutter…it's a lie!"

Again he grabbed her shoulders. "I stepped on a rock. I want a kiss. Shut your mouth and stick out your lips!"

She did, and he kissed her.

He reached up. "I'm holding the pipe. Molly." Now he hesitated. "Molly...you were scared a minute ago. You didn't know what to do when I grabbed your shoulders. You thought I might serve my desire...and not care about your feelings. Are you ready for hot water? I'm going to signal for it."

When he tapped the pipe, almost immediately he could feel it get warm, so he turned the valve enough to allow a small amount of water through.

"Yes, it's all right, Oliver. It's not too hot. You can open it."

He did. The water came down hard, in a stream only two or three inches wide. After ten or fifteen seconds passed he shut it off.

"I just got started!" she yelled.

"Get out!...and lather yourself. It's my turn."

Under it, he opened the valve and got thoroughly wet, then stepped aside, yelling..."I'll leave it on! Rinse off! Then get out!...and lather yourself!"

She did...then he went in and got wet, and stepped aside. "Get in and rinse off, then get out, and lather one more time."

When she finished her final rinsing, and stepped way, he went under again. But...the water stopped.

"What'll I do, Molly? The water is gone. My hair is full of soap."

"I didn't hear you...I'm drying off."

"This is terrible! Did you laugh? Molly..."

Then the water came again, and he rinsed.

He went to her. "Where's my towel? It was here...on this outside nail."

When she didn't answer, he reached for his flashlight. It was gone.

"Molly...!"

She laughed. "I knew more water was coming! Here's your flashlight!...and your stinky towel."

"It's your towel, I borrowed. Well...thanks for it, and for the entertainment."

"You were mean to me. I made you pay!"

"I wasn't mean. Well...maybe a bit insensitive."

"Oliver...I think you care about me...in a way I only hoped for. I mean...I did expect you to be kind, but I wasn't sure just how kind. But...I would have let you do it even if I was not wanting to. I choose to wait, but I would have done it. Because I love you."

"If I did it...maybe you would've loved me more, and liked me less."

They went back up to the outer door, and the Sherpa lady let them in. As they walked near to the dining room, he opened the door to it and said "Have a good night. We'll be on the trail at seven in the morning."

"Sure you will!" said Greg Barton. "Say 'nighty-night' to Molly for us."

There was a moment of silence in the room, followed by muffled laughter.

Marlaine said "Will you marry my sister?"

"Yes," he said.

She put her hand on her chest. "Well, then...say 'Nighty-night' to her."

Upstairs, in their room, he locked the door. He secured the window, and hung his parka from the bolt at the top of it, so it covered the glass. Then, lighting two candles...he put them on the window sill.

When he turned to Molly, who had zipped the bags together, she was standing beside the bed, looking at him.

The she looked down and, unzipping her parka, took it off and threw it to the other bed.

Before she showered she wore a black sweater. Now she had on her red one.

He stepped to her, and they embraced and kissed.

"It's cold," he said. "Twenty degrees, maybe. Get those clothes off!"

"Why? So you can study blue skin?"

"No!...so we can lay them on this other bunk...to get 'em on quickly in the morning. It'll be about fifteen degrees then."

"Well, turn around!"

"I'll close my eyes."

She said "No! I'm shy this first time."

He turned around.

"Never mind!" she said. "I want you to look. My skin is blue and hard...but look, anyway! So you'll know the truth."

He did. He faced her.

She pulled her sweater up...over her head.

Her bra was black.

"Your bra was pink. I mean you had on a pink one before you took the shower."

"How did you know?"

Now she dropped her hiking pants, and stood looking at him. It was cold in the room, but she blushed. Reaching down, she hooked her thumbs inside the black underpants and, pulling the edges away from her body, flashed herself to his view...then she shuddered, her whole body shaking... and leaped onto the bed. She got quickly into the bags.

He laughed. "Congratulations! But I already knew what you look like naked. I've undressed you many times…in the light and in the dark."

Her bra went flying by, landing on the other bunk.

"Oliver…you don't speak Nepali."

She laughed, and ducked her head into the bags.

He went to the window sill and blew out one of the candles.

"That's not fair! I undressed with both of them on."

He struck a match and lit the candle.

"Now go back to where you were standing. Right in front of me. I did it. You can do it!"

He went there and began to undress.

"You're wearing longjohns…for this special time?"

"In Kathmandu I wasn't expecting this, Anyway, don't judge me by my underwear."

"But, you look silly!" She laughed. "Take them off!"

He buttoned them slowly from the top. "What if, after they're off, you think I look silly?"

"Oliver, stop!"

"Stop undressing…?"

"No! Get undressed!"

"Molly…have you ever thought of me naked?

"Of course I have. In Namche…before you said "Hello" to me. When you were walking down the hill. And after that, many times."

"What about now?"

"I can see your blue body, shivering it's ass off…the way I had to. Yes."

He took off his longjohns and put them on the other bed.

She laughed. "But...I didn't know your butt was that shapely. I thought you didn't have one."

He put his clothes in two piles...for in the morning.

She said "Your back is ridged, like a sea shell. Well, why not?" Again she laughed. "I didn't know anyone had muscles like that. You're strong! Skinny, too...but now I can see why you were able to whip Bush."

As he folded his longjohns, which he almost never did, he said "When I was seven...and my brother nine...two little girls invited us to a house. The parents were away. So we went upstairs to this big room that had nothing in it except a bed...way on the other side of the room from the door. There was this big open space. And we decided that each one of us had to run...naked...across the floor...to the bed. One at a time. Skinny little things...leaping...laughing and being laughed at. Then...when we got to the bed, none of us knew what to do." He laughed. "I'll never forget it!"

He turned and walked toward her.

"Holy mackerel!" she said. "Nothing to laugh at there! I mean...that's something to not laugh at!" She laughed. "That's what I felt in the dark!...you tricked me! Every time we passed in the night...you banged me with it!"

"I had to have it there!" he said. "It doesn't scuttle about. It doesn't lay flat like lips."

"Breasts would be a better comparison," she said. "And... you didn't say anything about mine."

"They're beautiful, Molly. I remember them. Yes, they're blue!"

As he leaped onto the bed, she turned away from him, and made the opening of the bags tight around her neck.

"Molly...don't let me freeze! I was kidding. Your breasts are pink. Let me in...and I'll warm them."

"They're already warm. Go down and sleep with the yaks."

At that, she turned until she was on her back, and looked at him. Then she pushed away the bags from her neck.

He got in beside her, pulled the bags close, and then, reaching under her lower back, rolled her so that she was on top of him.

"You know what you want, Oliver."

He hugged her, and they kissed. Then he gently massaged her back.

She said "A little harder...in that spot. There! Ahh! Your strong hands can do it."

She began to punch his chest muscles with her knuckles.

"That feels good, Molly...in a way. Is it a form of torture?"

"I'm massaging you! Don't you like it?"

"Oh!...I love it, Molly. Drive them in, sweetheart!"

She leaned forward on him.

"Molly, I like your hair in my face. It's soft and comfy."

"Can you feel my things on your chest?"

He laughed. "What things?"

She sighed, and put her cheek against his.

"Ah...Molly...they're not blue now. Roll over, sweetheart, I need to be on top of you so I can see your eyes better."

She got off, and he got on her, and looked into her eyes.

"Will you marry me?"

"Yes!"

"Molly…here it is!…that place between our eyes."
"Yes!"
"Are you here?"
"Yes. It's a warm, light place, Oliver. It feels great. I love us together. And…I'm not just a pair of lips."

He said "Two lips and an oyster shell. There's more to this than eyes can tell."

He bent down and kissed her soft lips. Then she grabbed his butt cheeks, and squeezed. So he put her on top again, and squeezed hers.

It was four o'clock in the morning before they rested, and Molly dozed off. Her arm was outside the bags, so he tucked it in, the air being so cold. Then he kissed her cheek, and settled down to sleep.

CHAPTER THIRTEEN

"We're nearly to Pheriche," he said, as he took off his pack and leaned back against the resting place, a rock wall. "Actually, it's a couple hours away…but I didn't expect to be this far by noon."

Molly was having difficulty with a pack strap caught on the shoulder of her jacket, so he helped her.

"Molly, it's noon. You can speak to me, as you said you would. And yet…you look away! Sweetheart, I know it was hard to get up, but don't be mad! We can leave Curt far behind."

She yawned, then dozed, and her body moved slowly sideways.

Putting his arms around her, he pulled her to him. "Rest your head against me."

She did. Then she gently said "Oliver, I'm not angry. I'm tired. But I seem to be waking up, so let's get on with it."

Near to them was a small Nepali household, mostly of rock and old lumber. The thatched roof had dozens of rocks on it to hold it against a wind.

In front of it sat an upside-down, woven grass basket, covering two fully grown chickens. The lady of the house and a boy about three had appeared, and the boy lifted the basket, releasing the birds. After the mother captured and covered them, she scolded the boy. But suddenly he did it again, causing the lady to shriek, and scamper, and catch, and again basket them. She got a stick and spanked the boy, making him cry. The she hugged.

"She hates what he did, but loves him," Oliver said. "What if a stranger freed her chickens? As she beat him... and afterward...how much compassion would she feel?"

"Molly said "Like giving a man a cigarette before you execute him? I don't know. Is the stranger childlike...and does he cry?"

Oliver said "The lady loved the boy as she chased the chickens, and as she spanked. So, she knew the tears were there, and she would have known it even if he didn't cry then. Molly, do you think humans are born with integrity? If the light of the soul is clear then...are we all the same then...when we're born?"

"I believe we are," she said.

He asked "In the worst of humanity, is there yet a tiny light inside that can't go out?"

"Oliver....even if you knew it...would you give Hitler a cigarette?"

He didn't answer for a minute or two...just looked away, occasionally scratching his cheek.

"Love is why we have ethics, Molly. But…if I'm facing a stranger, and I offer a cigarette, perhaps I'm honoring my conclusions about what ought to be loved. If I never felt love for that stranger, in the sense of having been with his inner innocence, how could I have compassion for him?"

"Your kindness would be necessary, but distant? What if his mother and father were there?"

"If they loved him, once…they'd love him still," he said. "And maybe they'd pass the feeling to me."

He deeply sighed. "But…otherwise, what is love?"

"Don't fret, Oliver. John Finn told me your sense of kindness would get you knocked down sometimes. But isn't that the right way to live?"

"Molly, we just saw the lady trying to teach that to her boy. Nah!...she was just loving him. Maybe that's all the ethics you need. But…how do you feel it for a stranger?"

"Anyway, Oliver…do we believe the same way about God?"

"Molly…I feel there is a center of awareness…as the "I" in my head, is "I" everywhere in it. God, or the "I" of Consciousness…is "Here"…everywhere."

She said "But I think God cares about me."

"Molly, I think in this universe freewill dominates fate. And yet…I always felt each of us has a path we ought to be on. There's something "just there", directing…in a way we don't understand."

She reached over and put her hand on his forehead, and brushed aside some hair.

"What were you thinking last night…after we got married, and you ate my little underpants?"

"I didn't!...I tricked you...made you think I did." He laughed. "What were you thinking when you yelled "Holy Mackerel...this is it!...?"

He got up and, after she did, too, hugged her. And they both laughed.

"Let's go!" And he quickly put on his pack, then began moving away.

Turning to her and smiling, he said "I don't care what the yaks think...you're the one for me."

"But...you failed to hug me!"

He hugged her.

After awhile they came to a place where they could look ahead into a large, barren valley, with a handful of houses on both sides of a straight trail.

"This isn't Pangboche," he said.

She said "And so...why isn't this Pangboche?"

"Because that place is under big pines, on the side of a gently rising hill. You would have loved it. At the monastery the monks have a pointed scalp, they call a yeti. We'll stop on the way down."

"I know where it is, Oliver. It was above us...when the lady was spanking the boy. What's this place?"

"Pheriche."

"Why do you assume I don't like this valley? Can anything live in it worth eating?"

"Molly...look! Patches of old grass. There are places higher than this, where villagers take cattle in summer for grazing. There'll be a small, stone enclosement...and larger, rock-walled areas...all of which they call a karka. There's some over this rise."

He pointed ahead.

She leaned against him. "This is where I want to be, Oliver. Thanks for bringing me here. And I'll go to Changri La with you…and stand in the snow of that highest place."

They walked onward a hundred feet or so, along the easy, straight trail.

Molly said "What's that sign?...beside the trail ahead?" She pointed. "It was just put there."

They came to a wooden post. It was driven in, but also the ground had been dug, because the dirt was freshly turned, and some of the dirt had been placed firmly around the wood, perhaps tamped by a boot. Attached to it, near the top, was a piece of rusty tin about a foot long and six inches wide.

Someone scraped the metal, and wiped it, making it red-colored. Rusty. On it was black lettering. They went to it and read.

Did you say you want to live
your own life? Ha, ha, ha.
I'm laughing. Can you hear me?

Oliver pulled out the post and sign, and flung the entire thing. It went beyond the edge of an incline, disappearing from their sight.

He didn't speak. He hugged Molly, and moved onward.

CHAPTER FOURTEEN

In Pheriche he took Molly into a long, one-story building whose porch nearly touched the trail. They stepped to the left, crossed the porch, then went down stairs about six feet.

Oliver pointed to his left, "There's the dormitory."

That room was about twenty feet long, and twelve wide, with six double bunks against the wall away from the trail.

"Someone is sleeping there," she said. "On the lower bunk at the end...in that red bag."

Turning to the right, he led her into the kitchen, where two women were standing at the center of it, near a rock and clay fireplace-stove. This was a smaller room, with four tables, two of which were against the wall closest to the trail.

"Namaste!" he said. "Can we rent a bunk?"

An old woman was there, who was busy cooking. A younger lady, thin and tall, with glasses, touched her hands together, and held them high, and smiled. "You've been here before. Put your packs in the dorm and choose a bed. Come back for tea." Then she quickly found a notebook, and handed it to him. "But now you have a wife?" She looked at Molly.

"Yes…this is Molly."

When the lady put out her right hand, Molly took it. The old lady at the stove, nodded.

He said "Only one other person has come?"

The younger, thin lady whispered "This one is taller than most…and seems strong…but he is lady-like. He walks like this." She moved a few short, dainty steps.

"He's sleeping," said Oliver. "Have you seen a tall, tough man? Boom boom."

The lady looked at him but didn't answer. She put two fingers to her lips, and widened her eyes.

"My dearest, Oliver," said Molly. "You do speak Nepali, I would guess…and know a hundred times more than I do. But…"boom, boom" means balloon."

"It does? So…when those pretty girls looked at me and said "Boom, boom" and I thought they meant I was tough, they were saying I looked like a balloon? Sure!...I was wearing a puffy parka."

"Poor Oliver!" said Molly, laughing. "You thought the girls wanted to marry you."

And now the thin lady was smiling.

"So…" he said, "Have you seen a tall, blond man, who walks like this?" He puffed up his chest and walked a few steps.

"Boom, boom?" the lady asked.

"No! Tough. Strong."

"Yes!" the lady said. "In my dreams…just last night."

She laughed, and the old lady did, too, rocking back and forth in a chair.

"No!" said Oliver. "The blond man is bad. He likes to murder."

The ladies stopped laughing, and looked at him, but they didn't speak.

He thought perhaps they were unfamiliar with the word "murder", so he put his hands together, as though around a throat. "He loves to kill."

The thin lady got nearer to them, and spoke in a low tone. "Yes, a tall, blond man. He came, and stood there, near the bottom step. He looked at the beds, two minootes…then at me." She put hand to her throat as though protecting it, "I went for a menu book…and then he was gone. When I looked again, he was nowhere. I went outside but didn't see him. Perhaps he was already walking beyond the clinic, and heading for Lobuche."

Motioning with his hand toward the dorm, he asked "What color is this man's hair?"

"I don't know…he wore a hat. But this man is not the other."

Oliver wrote ~~is~~ HIS menu, and handed it to the lady.

Molly moved to her and peeked at the words. "Sherpa stew?…and an omelet with cheese? Is that yak cheese?"

"You don't like it?"

"I love it!"

The lady smiled. "Yes, of course. You're his wife."

Molly said "But…I just happen to love it. I don't need to."

"She speaks of destiny, Molly," said Oliver. "Not servility. It's a compliment to us."

A Sherpa entered and, from the top step, began speaking to the lady. He was telling her about his clients, who were sitting on the porch. He said they were in poor condition and wouldn't enter. Would she please bring tea, and menus.

Oliver had seen him before, on the trail. "Namaste!" he said. "Tapainglai sangshai hunahan chha?"

The man answered, smiling, "Ma sangchai chhu.

Hello. How are you? You speak Nepali good…now."

They shook hands.

Oliver said "You come from Lobuche?"

"From Tukla," the man replied, looking downward. "We move slowly."

"I hope your friends get better. Did you see a tall, blond man?" He waved his arms toward the north. "An hour away. Ek ghanttaa. Maybe half hour."

The Sherpa didn't answer, but pursed his mouth and closed his eyes.

Oliver added "With a dark green parka. And probably he didn't speak to you. He's unfriendly."

The man opened his eyes. "Oh, yes. A half hour. Saaddha. He looked at the ground as he walked."

In the dorm, after leaning their packs against the trailside wall, they stepped to the opposite side, and went between the third and fourth set of bunks, counting from the south end and the sleeping man.

Oliver put his bag on the bottom of the third row, and Molly put hers beside him, in the fourth.

"Please put yours above me, Molly."

Before she could answer, Greg Barton arrived. He had paused at the bottom steps and nodded to the ladies, then brought his gear to the row of bunks beyond Molly... kitchen-side. Norm entered, followed by Marlaine, Bush, and Marlaine's porter.

It seemed to Oliver that the only one painfully tired was Norm

Now, as the others considered where to sleep, Molly moved to the bunk above Oliver, and Greg Barton moved to where Molly had been. Then Norm insisted that Marlaine take the one Greg had been on, and he took the next bottom one. And the final row, at the kitchen wall, had Bush at the bottom, with Marlaine's porter expected to sleep at the top.

Norm told the porter to do that, but the young man didn't go to it.

Greg Barton spoke quietly to Norm and Marlaine. "The porter will feel comfortable...below, at the outer wall."

"I'd like to have him on the upper bunk. So I can know where he is."

The porter had already stepped to the row of packsacks against that wall, and was clearing a place to sleep. He had a blanket.

Norm spoke commandingly to the porter. "You don't have a sleeping bag?"

Oliver said "He got a blanket from the lady. Let him sleep where he's comfortable."

"Dammit!" said Norm. "He'll need a bag, above...up where it's zero. That's Marlaine's porter."

"But, Norm…he didn't know he was going "above". When you go to the talk at the clinic, tell them you need a porter for yourself, and two sleeping bags."

"I'll do what I please!" said Norm

"So will the porter," Oliver answered, calmly. "And I'll support him! But, of course, you would have rented him a bag in Namche…wouldn't you, Norm…if you bothered to ask him about it."

"He should have told me!" Norm snorted.

"The man seems shy," said Oliver. "And…as I said, he didn't know you might need him beyond Lobuche."

Without a word Norm departed, banging his boots loudly on the stair steps.

Oliver got partly into his bag. "I'll just rest briefly, Molly."

The man at the end, who was entirely in his bag, now spoke faintly, apparently only to Oliver, in a high but gentle voice. "Will you go to Everest?"

"No. We're going west of Gorak Shep, from Kala Patar."

"I've seen the map," said the man.. "There's Shangrila, you know. You can go there and forget this life and never grow old."

Oliver said "If you want to forget this life, you can do it here…by killing what's bad in your head."

In a minute, the man said, yet speaking gently, "Yes, boss. And will the old man go, too? I'm Frankie Monahan."

"I'm Oliver Faulkner. He wants to turn eastward, to Everest base camp, and go over Lho La into Tibet. Often that's a desire we don't quite define…but which pulls us…all our ignorant lives." Oliver sighed…then he softened his tone. "Sorry! I seem to be in a bad mood. Maybe it's the altitude."

He lay back, and covered himself until only his face was out.

"Molly." He spoke lowly, sure that she was napping above him. There was no response from her. Also...everyone else was quiet.

For a minute he breathed deeply, wanting to make it a habit, at this higher place. Then he remembered what happened in Lobuche the last time he was above. He had taken a top bunk at the rock-wall end of the dorm, unaware that the kitchen stove was on the other side of it. Which wouldn't have mattered if expedition porters weren't on strike, resulting in a fire which burned slowly almost the entire night. And so, the wood was smoldering...was smoking. And he was breathing deeply, purposely...in the blackness of the room...and not knowing why his heart seemed to be flipping...but blaming it on altitude...until someone turned on a candle and he could see the smoke.

Now he was blaming something else on altitude. His irritation. He almost never got angry for no apparent reason, until on the way down...usually below Namche.

He was now aware that the man had turned toward him. In the short distance, about nine feet, the movement was peripherally obvious; and Oliver looked, hoping to see the face. He saw the top of a head, and a watchcap.

"Are you feeling healthy?" Oliver asked.

"Yes, thank you." It was a high, dim voice.

The politeness was beginning to irritate Oliver. But he blamed himself for having that feeling.

"You are alert, but you may lack awareness of your physical self. Do you think you're strong...or do you think you're weak?"

"Strong…but tired."

Oliver said "You speak as though you're far away. Do you have a headache or feel swollen in the head?

"No."

"What of your coordination and speed of response. Raise your feet inside the bag."

And…after some hesitation it was done.

The man made a clicking sound in his mouth. "I'm all right."

"Apparently. And…even though you paused when I asked you to raise your legs, I assume you're not sick. Do you feel guilty about hiding?"

"Yes. But I need to hide. Thank you for seeing it. And don't worry…my kind, new friend…I'll come out tomorrow. Then I'll do what you said, maybe."

"What did I say to do?"

The man laughed. "You advised me to kill what's in my head."

"Do you have an appetite?"

"For what?"

"Food!" Oliver said.

"Yes. I'll eat later. And who are you…at the top? Oh, I remember…Oliver."

"Oliver Faulkner. And my love is with me." Again he felt angry…and figured he shouldn't be. "Her name is Molly."

Oliver didn't sleep. In awhile he got up and, after kissing Molly's cheek as she slept, sat on the edge of the bed and began to fasten a knife to his staff.

"That's a khukari," said Norm, having come back, in a way unaware to Oliver. "The traditional knife of Nepal."

Marlaine said "They know that!"

Molly appeared from above, coming down to sit on the bed beside him. She watched him work.

So did the others watch.

Greg Barton said "You're using twine Of course, as a fisherman you know how. Have you been in the military, Oliver?"

"A couple years…in the army."

"And you had bayonet training?"

"Yes. My instructor just retired. I read in the news that one of his trainees attacked him, so he killed him."

"You sound proud of it!" Molly said.

He said "Whatever you learn…it might as well have been taught by the best."

Bush said "Were you in the military, Mr. Barton?"

"Yes. During the Korean War."

"But you weren't in…huh, Norm?" said Bush.

"No! Neither were you!"

"I was just asking. Not looking for trouble."

Oliver said "Where are you from, Norm?"

He was almost certain he knew the answer, but had asked in an easy manner, wanting to be friendly.

Norm was obviously irritated. He looked away. "You know I'm Jewish…and from New York City. And to be specific…"

He didn't finish.

Bush got up. "I'm going in for tea. Are you coming? Anyone? Old man?…did you order din din?"

Greg got up. And Norm did. As Marlaine followed, she said "Molly, come in…please! I need to talk with you."

Molly said "Yes", then leaned against Oliver. She whispered "That's because she can't talk with Norm. Maybe she wants to go home."

He waited until Norm and Marlaine were away a bit. "Think she might?"

"She'll probably ditch him...sometime."

"Yeh...he needs to be pushed over edges, in order to get ice melted...by someone who cares to do it."

She asked "Are you coming in for tea?"

"I'll be there soon...in three or four minutes. After I finish this spear."

"Do you love me?"

"Why would I have stopped?"

"Oliver...kiss me!"

He did.

⇥✢⇤

She went into the kitchen, so he worked on his spear. When it was finished he set it aside.

The man at the end said "Wouldn't you be nice...to tell the lady I want fried rice with chicken. Thank you, so. She can put it on my stool. Anyway...you and Molly have a lovely night. Kissy...kissy...before it ends...at the killing time."

"I assume," said Oliver, "You mean when emptiness is put to death."

"Oh, yes," said the man.

"But...of course, it isn't!" Oliver said. "It's only put to sleep."

In the kitchen, everyone except the porter and Molly sat at the immediate table, past the stairs. Bush, Greg, Marlaine and Norm were having tea and toast.

"Where's Molly?" he asked. "It's getting toward dark."

"Out back," said Marlaine/ "She had to pee. Oh, don't worry! That tall Sherpa lady went with her. And remember…Curt was seen far away, leaving town. It's all right!"

He sat at the other table, but at the near end. Then he noticed the porter sitting beyond the stove, talking to the old lady. And he was glad everyone was here…and safe. Except that Molly was outside.

A map was laid out on the table, before Greg Barton and Marlaine.

Greg said "This is Lho La…above Everest base camp. The Nepal-China border is there."

"I need to check on Molly," said Oliver.

"Oh, my!" said Marlaine, leaning over the map. "On the other side of it is a jumbly glacier. You can't go that way!"

Molly and the Sherpa lady entered, and Molly came to stand beside him. He put his arm under her parka, and held her waist, and she leaned against him.

"Rongbuk," said Norm, also leaning toward the map. "That's the name of the glacier. They climb Everest from there, sometimes."

"But I've decided to go with you," said Greg Barton. "Not to your mountain, but to your pass. Is this it, Oliver? Changri La?"

Marlaine said "Oliver, what's it like there, at that pass?"

"Just a snowy, walled pass, I suppose."

Greg said "It's about nineteen thousand feet."

"But…you've never been there, Oliver?" asked Marlaine.

"I only looked that way, from Gorak Shep. And it seemed that you can walk across the glaciers. Changri Shar. Shar means east…"

Norm said "The sharpas, or sherpas, came from the northeast."

"Then we'd move onto Changri Nup…and go along it's edge, as we head west. About three miles. Then north a mile or so to Changri La."

Norm said "If you haven't been there…why should we follow you?"

Greg Barton said "Because he's the leader."

Marlaine leaned over, again. "Changri Nup. How do you know we can walk on it?"

"I don't! But others have been…for centuries. We'll have to look at it."

Molly said "Oliver has a better map than that. It's a topographical one."

"Yes, I do…but we'll only know about the place when we get there."

Greg said "I'll go to that pass with you. Not beyond it. Norm and Bush want this mountain?...it looks like a tough six days, from the pass and back. I have no need for that."

"I was thinking four days," said Oliver, glancing at Norm and Bush. "You two could go over this hill, at the edge of town." He pointed east. "And head northeast to Imj Tse. It's twenty thousand feet…and said to be an easy one. You can do that in four days, probably…from here and back. But… you're the ones who started this trip, so if you really want to go beyond Changri La, I'll take you."

"I might just go to Imja Tse!" snorted Norm. "Island Peak, they call it. What about you, Bush? Want to go with me?"

Bush hesitated, then said "I've become rather fond of these people. I...what about you, Marlaine?"

She said "I think this world is mine only to a point, and I'm almost to it...maybe. But I'll go toward that pass with Molly and them."

There was silence. Then Oliver said "Norm...Imja Tse is often climbed. It might be better for you because you'd see a trail. Ahh!...it's tough getting onto the right path. Make your choice...then relax and enjoy it. If it's a failure...so be it."

Greg Barton said "How can you pick up wisdom without being knocked down, now and then? Also, when the student is ready, the teacher will appear."

"That's thousands of years old!" snapped Norm.

Again it was quiet.

Bush said, lightheartedly, "Marlaine...when you're way up here, there's no one to steal from except your friends. So, that's good, isn't it?"

Oliver remembered about the request from the man in the dorm...for fried rice with chicken. He told the lady.

Greg Barton said "At least he wants to eat. Maybe he's hiding because of fear. That's not a crime."

Marlaine said "Perhaps he's shy by nature."

"But...what is he doing here, in this world?" said Norm.

"Harsh, but beautiful," Oliver said. "The ladies seem to enjoy it, too."

"Then it's not a place to hide," said Norm.

"Any place is!" Molly said. "If you're afraid in it. She should bring him the rice and chicken…and not force him to come out."

Oliver said "Maybe he's just living his own life. He's here and not here."

"What can he gain by being here?" asked Norm.

"I don't know!" Oliver said. "But…if he wears his parka with hood up, and a face mask…he can yet see what he wants to see and do what he wants to do, or try to do. He can see the sun on the highest mountain."

Molly put her hand on his. "He can go to the highest place he's ever been."

Greg Barton said "It could be that he's looking for something he's afraid to find. Maybe something he lost." Now he laughed. "So am I. In my case it's what I loved…my wife…and another world, in which she and I played. It's just beyond my reach."

Molly said "We don't know that man. Let's stop talking about him."

"She's right!" Oliver defended.

Greg Barton nodded in agreement.

Bush said "But it makes you feel uncomfortable, when a man seems to be hiding."

"Ah…crap! He's just tired!" Norm said.

It was getting dark so the old lady brought candles to the tables, and lit them. The tall daughter served Greg Barton rice with lentil soup.

Molly whispered to Oliver. "Did they serve him first because he's the oldest?"

"Probably," he whispered back. "But...only he, Bush and the porter are having dal bhaat."

Greg Barton said "Don't whisper!...unless you're being romantic...then it's OK."

The Sherpa lady carried a dish and candles into the dormitory.

Oliver said "She's bringing Curt his food."

Everyone else seemed to be holding their breath. Bush got up from his position closest to the dorm and walked toward Oliver's table. "What did you say? Do you think it's Curt?"

"No! I wanted you all to take the possibility into awareness. We've thought it, then dismissed it. The lady said he's far away. My Sherpa guide friend, who stopped here, thought he saw Curt walking toward Lobuche."

Norm said "If you think it isn't him, why are you scaring us?"

"If any danger exists you ought to acknowledge its possibility. Yes, Curt was seen leaving, and seen far away. And, beside this man's apparent feminine character, reposing cocoon-like...a questionable situation...is one which seems unquestionable. Why jump into the inner bunk, if it could be like choosing to land on a spider's web?"

Marlaine said "You mean...why would he take such a chance at getting caught?"

Greg Barton wondered "What are you suggesting we do, Oliver?"

The Sherpa lady returned, and Oliver said "Excuse me, is the man eating?"

"Yes, I put a candle on a chair, and his food on a bench. He's eating."

"Did you see his face?"

"No. I saw hair. Short yellow hair. The other man..." She waved toward the north. "Had blond hair. This is not the other man."

After putting a hand to her throat, she returned to the stove.

Oliver said "As Bush pointed out...it's the mystery of a man hiding. Certainly that man isn't Curt. But...if any of you want to move to a different hotel, go ahead. I'll stay here. I'm the one to blame for this feeling of danger."

"I wouldn't desert you," said Molly.

Norm said "This is dumb! Let's go pull him out of his bed! We can find out who he is!"

"No!" said Oliver. "That form...in the bed...has a right to privacy."

"That's true!" said Greg Barton. "We only know it's a human being. And so...I agree to do nothing now!"

Oliver lowered his voice. "I'll have Molly go to the bunk at this end, where the porter was told to be. I'll be in my row, but above, and I'll be loud...to let it be known I'm there. That'll take away the danger to any of you. But, Molly, you've got to be quiet about it."

"I prefer something more violent," said Norm. "Let's go get him!" He stood up, and looked down at Oliver. "I'm going in...to pull his hair."

Without looking up, Oliver said "Then...if the hair isn't Curt's, will you be sorry? Think of a way to see his face. Ask the Sherpa lady for help."

Norm went into the dorm, and everyone waited, listening. Then Norm came out with his packsack and sleeping bag. At the bottom step, he said "This is stupid! I'm leaving!"

Marlaine said "You're not in danger, Norm...Oliver is. We should stick together."

"If you leave," said Oliver, "I won't be angry. You have no need to deal with my problem. But I want you with us tomorrow. You're the one who got this trip started."

Norm returned to the dorm...soon reappearing without his pack and bag. "This is crap! I'm getting into bed. Anybody else?"

As the others went to their beds, Oliver walked to the far end. He sat on the bed next to the man, and said "How do you feel?"

There was no answer...except that he could hear deep breathing. He listened for pretended control of it, but this seemed relaxed, and naturally constant.

Without using his flashlight he returned to the third row and put his pack and parka on the lower bed, and his sleeping bag on the upper. Then...listening again, he could hear, even from that distance, about eight feet, the same deep breathing. So, feeling that the night would pass safely, he climbed up and got into his bag.

After a few minutes passed he remembered the spear. There seemed to be no danger but, wanting to assure safety to his friends, he unzipped the bag and climbed down to the floor. He had put the spear under the bottom bunk.

It was gone.

Again he went to the man's bed. He felt under it, and along the wall near it. When certain the breathing was as before, he felt around the bag. He found nothing.

He thought perhaps Norm took it.

Now he was disgusted that he cared who had it. Not trying to be quiet, he went to his bunk and got into his bag.

Then he hoped the man was Curt, and that he did have it. He said, aloud, "Let's fight!" Then he felt silly, figuring he said it to Frankie Monahan...who was metamorphosing in his bag.

He wondered if Molly heard him.

"I love you!" he said. Then he laughed. "I don't mean you!"

From the far end of the room, Molly said, in a tiny voice, "Do you mean me?"

"Yes."

Greg Barton said "I'm glad you don't mean me."

"Me, neither!" said Bush.

"What about me?" Marlaine said.

"Ah, shit!" said Norm. "I've heard enough!"

"Did you take my spear, Norm?"

There was a moment of silence.

"Oh, Oliver," came Molly's tiny voice. "Norm is scared, but...I think he wouldn't steal part of your defense."

After the room was quiet ten or fifteen minutes, and he thought everyone was sleeping, Molly thrust forward a whisper. "When are you coming to me, Oliver?"

He didn't answer, figuring it was too soon to accept that the night was safe. He loudly sighed, rolled over, and then breathed heavily, as though asleep.

Not wanting to be detected as pretending, he began to breathe more quietly. He moved so that his face was up, knowing he could hear better in that position.

He began to doze but tried not to...and saw a river, with mist, and sunshine entering in beams. And now at the very edge of regaining full consciousness, he saw cards on a table. When playing solitaire, sometimes as he prepared to move on, he'd sense an error, so he'd hesitate. Feeling blind, he was yet open. Then...he would see.

Taking a deep breath, he let out the air quickly, and relaxed. Then...he saw the missed play. That's when he heard the forced silence from the end of the room, and felt that the steadiness, earlier, also was forced.

Did Curt think he was found out? Or was the other man only listening in self defense?

There was a barely audible scraping sound at the end bunk, followed by silence. Then, not far from his head, came a light thump.

As adrenaline flooded through him, he turned to look.

The intense darkness of the room was touched by pale moonlight on the window. Moving across this was a tall man with a watch-cap, carrying a pack slung on one shoulder.

Oliver put his legs over the edge of the bed and, leaning forward, stared into the darkness.

He hesitated. Maybe this was only a man departing.

That's when a hand was put on his leg. It was a small hand, firmly but gently placed and, although he knocked it away, he knew it was Molly.

She whispered "Oliver, I thought I saw you walking. Was it that blond man? He had a pack...and then took it off!"

"Get under the lower bunk!" he whispered. Then he raised his voice. "Now!"

That's when Greg shouted "Who the hell are you?"

A flashlight was turned on, apparently Greg's, and it showed a form kneeling beside Norm's bunk, reaching under it. Yes, there was the spear. And now the man had it, and was lunging toward the light.

As Oliver landed on the floor, he saw and heard the flashlight hit the wood of the bunk above Greg. The light went out.

Now in the darkness was a louder, deeper thump. Then Greg said "Ahh! Ow!"

Bush shouted "I'm coming, man! Is it Curt?"

Oliver leaped toward the space between Greg's bunk and Norm's, but at the end of it he crouched and waited, expecting Bush's light to come on, or to get a clue in some other way about where, precisely, to attack.

"Mr. Barton is hurt!" Marlaine yelled. It seemed that she tried to muffle the sound, but it cut through.

"My hand hit the bunk! I'm all right!"

"I saw him get you!" she said.

"My bag is slashed!" said Barton. "Just get him!"

Oliver charged into the space between their bunks, and went entirely through it until he smashed against the back wall. So he hurried to his own bunk, thinking of Molly.

She was safe…underneath.

He ran back to Greg's row and, hearing a noise toward the outer wall, went that way…full ahead. He was expecting to get hit, and then to fight.

He smashed into the outer wall, as he tripped over a porter.

Bush's light came on.

There was no Frankie Monahan, and no Curt.

The door above the stairs was wide open.

CHAPTER FIFTEEN

It was cold and not yet to daylight, and it was snowing when they began climbing he hill at the end of town. Oliver was leading, with Molly near, then Greg Barton, Marlaine, Norm, the porter, and Bush.

But now, after about twenty minutes, they were arrived nearly at the top of the hill, where the trail turns northwest. And the day was dawning clearly.

Oliver yelled "This is almost fifteen HUNDRED feet, but in awhile the sun will make you take off your jacket. When you get in the shade...put it on. Just a word of caution." He cleared his throat. "Of course, I didn't need to say it to you, Greg."

Molly said "Thanks for saying it to me. When I arrive at shade, later, and get cold...now I'll know enough to put on my jacket, instead of standing there drooling, shivering, and grinning."

Sure, Molly. Glad to be of service. I'll be giving you more advice later. Particularly...if I see you grinning."

At mid-morning, Oliver could see a wooden building ahead, a bit below them, which he recognized as a place to get tea and biscuits. And he saw, among the four travelers standing in its yard, that one of them was Bhim Adjikari.

Oliver pointed, and spoke to Molly. "There's Bhim. A friend of mine. He's a guide."

"You have good eyesight," she said. "I can't see the faces, hardly."

After a pause, he said "If you were there, I would know it. Wouldn't you…if I were there?"

"Yes. So…he's a close friend."

Greg said "It's a good point. Seeing people you know… is much less confusing."

"Last night I failed to get at the truth early," said Oliver.

"I think you were being kind," Greg answered. "So you were opting for proper justice. But…maybe you were too kind. That's why you waited. As for Curt, ahead, remember that sometimes we identify what to hate…too late."

As they approached the building, his friend Bhim departed from it in a group of three. And when they met, he and Bhim stepped to the side of the trail, and bowed, then hugged one another.

"How are you, Bhim?"

"Fine, thanks. Tapainglai Pani?"

"Good! My friends and I intend to walk west of Gorak Shep, along Changri Nup Glacier. Maybe climb a mountain. I'll be going through Changri La."

Bhim said "Only one porter? In Lobuche you must get biscuits and noodles. Do you have fuel?"

Bhim's client had walked past them. Now he yelled back. "Let's move! I'm not paying you to chat!"

Bhim didn't attend directly, but turned to the porter and told him to follow the client.

Has he been this way from the beginning?" Oliver asked.

Bhim bowed deeply, with his hands held high. He said "From the beginning."

"It's too bad you have to listen to him. But I know you must.

"Or I would have trouble with my trekking agency."

"It doesn't bother you much, anyway…does it."

Bhim shrugged his shoulders, and smiled. "Not much."

"Bhim, did you see a tall, blond man?"

"Yes. He goes west of Gorak Shep…as you. He asked me directions. I told him "No!"…that he must return to Kathemandu."

"Why?"

"He's crazy!" said Bhim. "His eyes were filled with nothing he was looking at. And he had a crying eye."

"Do you think he's sad?"

"No…he got hit. His eye was red."

The client was yelling, so they shook hands and Bhim departed.

Oliver went to the building, where the others were outside of it, drinking tea.

Bush said "Why didn't Curt try to kill you in Namche? The crazy ass is losing places to hide. No more trees? Not many buildings."

Norm asked "How many buildings are in Lobuche? One?"

"At least six," he answered. "Every time I get there, I see a couple more. I don't know. Anyway, I'll search them…

now thinking about Curt. And I can walk ahead, alone, for awhile."

Bush said "Why be alone, pal? I'll be near."

"Thanks, Bush."

"And you'll let him?" asked Molly.

"Yes. If he chooses to."

"I'll be by your side," she said.

"I'm glad."

Norm said "And you'll let her? I'd want to be clear of that hindrance. And I wouldn't want anyone close behind me. Who wants to think there's someone closely following?"

"Oliver..." Marlaine began in a tone more intimate than usual. "Do you believe that what is behind you, of the past, can indicate success to what is ahead?"

Molly said "She means "fate". The life behind...has a guiding part, we think...as it is part of your fate. You can be more confident in your expectations."

"Yes," said Marlaine. "You and Molly belong together. So...you will win, won't you?"

"What he thinks is this..." snapped Norm. "God only winds it up, and doesn't give a damn what happens afterward."

"Norm...you're giving God the feelings of a man," said Oliver. "I think God is the clock...not separate from it. Also, I think the nature of existence, even in apparent chaos, is harmonic. But..."

Greg Barton said "What he's brought to this point, hallmarks his character, and shows what's likely to happen. But...he can't say who will win."

Marlaine said "The person who does bad things ought to lose!"

Molly said "Oliver, you told me that several times during your life you seemed, clearly, to be in the hands of fate. You seemed outside yourself...beyond yourself. You were being empty...loving only...in the way you can be when thoughtlessly before a rose."Well..." She raised her shoulder. "I think you have a path, and when you're on it, God allows you to be before a rose."

Greg Barton said "Sometimes people die when you think they shouldn"t."

"Children die," said Bush.

Marlaine said "But...when you meet Curt, wouldn't you like to feel certain about winning?"

"He'll be confident," said Greg Barton. "Also...he won't under-rate his enemy. But even if he did feel uncertain, he would yet have courage."

Oliver said "And the courage we're pointing at...is of defending life in the name of goodness. If harmony is the basis of existence, inclusive of seeming chaos, the result of the fight was perhaps determined at the beginning of purpose. Yes, I think you're right. As to what is permanent, I can't lose and Curt can't win.

But...he can live and I can die."

Molly said "I believe in a personal God...one who cares about you, in particular. And because you're a good man, Oliver, he'll watch over you, and help you."

Marlaine said "I agree with my sister."

"So do I!" said Bush.

"And yet...if I die, nothing of love will change," said Oliver.

He stood up and put on his pack.

"I'll be behind you, too," said Marlaine. "Are you coming, Norm?"

"I'll be along, in my own time."

Bush said "I'll walk with you, Marlaine. How far is it, Oliver?"

"An hour..maybe two."

As Oliver walked, after a half hour he was a bit ahead. On a winding trail, along which he usually saw a couple hundred feet either way, the others were out of sight. Now at a place he could see almost straight down to Khumbu Glacier, and the steep rise to his left began at his shoulder, he would rest a minute, and wait for them.

Then he saw a hooded figure about three hundred feet ahead, at the end of a slight west-swing arc. A man was moving along, and was almost to where the trail got very near to the glacier again.

Oliver went quickly onward, walking…until the man disappeared around a bend…and then he ran, as well as his pack would allow.

When he got to the bend he could see another three hundred feet of the trail, in a westward arc. And there, away half that distance, at mid-arc, was Curt. With his hood down, he was looking at debris in the trail, which had come from above. There was a jumble of snow and rocks, some of the rocks quite large, two being boulder size.

Probably a large volume of powdery snow had fallen, far above, with enough force to cause this.

Beyond Curt a Nepali family of four was approaching, and was nearly to the debris. A man with a heavy dokha, the load causing him to take short, rushing steps, during which he leaned upon his staff, was leading a woman with a toddler in her basket. Her load was partly supported by a tumpline around her forehead. And there was a child, a boy, of three or four, at his mother's heels.

The man now stopped and rested on the crosspiece of his staff. The wife put her stick against a pile of dirt at the side of the hill. The boy suddenly ran ahead.

The boy went to the nearest boulder to him. It was the larger of the two, although both were about three feet across. The other boulder was just a couple steps beyond, on the inner part of the trail, near Curt.

As the boy found his place at the rock, Curt glanced that way, then again looked toward the ground near himself. Now his eyes went to the outer edge of the trail, where nothing was.

Oliver remembered Bhim speaking of what Curt was seeing.

Suddenly Molly's voice was behind him.

"What will you do, Oliver?"

Then...there was a loud sound from above, as of something heavy thumping the hill...following a salvo of distant rumbles which perhaps wouldn't have entered his consciousness without the thump.

He saw that the others, at the middle of the arc, were looking upward.

Molly was now leaning against him.

"What'll we do?" yelled Molly.

"Nothing! Don't move, sweetheart."

At a bend, he and Molly were under a wedge-shape area, which promised to avert debris.

It was very quiet. Then he noticed another Nepali family standing beyond the first...observing...and looking upward.

Curt ran toward the boy's boulder and, when almost to it, thrust himself forward, diving to the shelter of it. Then he lay there against the flat outer surface.

The boy was watching him, and he was standing no more than three feet from where Curt came to hide. Then the boy looked upward, and stepped closer to Curt, so that he was about two feet away. He kneeled in that spot.

The mother yelled...told the boy to get closer to the rock.

All Curt needed to do was reach out and pull in the child.

He didn't.

Of the dozen or so pieces of falling ice and rock, some were larger than a man's head, and one of those hit the boy in the head. There was no doubt, to Oliver, that he was instantly killed.

"I'm going to the boulder, Molly."

The mother had acted as the rocks were falling and, even as Oliver began to walk, she was arriving. Then the father did. Now she was holding the boy and looking at his head.

Both parents had shed their packs. The father, now unburdened by his, took the boy and, without a word, moved along the trail...perhaps having in mind the doctors in Pheriche. When he came to Oliver, his eyes were wet...also, he seemed to be unaware of the man he glanced at.

The other Nepalis, a man and two ladies, had run to the mother, and one of the ladies tried to hold her, perhaps only to give comfort, but she broke loose and went to her pack in which the toddler sat and, putting it on, moved away…also without a word. She was looking at the ground as she passed her friends.

Oliver stopped when she got to him, and he bowed his head to show sadness. She didn't look at him, directly, but pursed her mouth to acknowledge his understanding.

Of the three other Nepalis, the man was at the boulder, watching the departing parents, and the women were now about twenty feet beyond, and attending to Curt who had moved along to the outer edge of things. He was looking down at the glacier.

Oliver knew the Nepali man. The first time he came into the mountains, Bhim had stopped on the trail and conversed with him.

"Namaste!" said Oliver. "Will they take the boy to Pheriche?"

"To their home in Orsho."

Now one of the women was screaming at Curt. And one of the things she said was "Why didn't you save the boy?"

Curt looked downward, along the glacier, up and down it, as though enjoying the view, and having no interest in considering her question.

Oliver's Sherpa friend, after turning to face the scene, shouted "We don't want you in Nepal. I'll be seeing the army in Pheriche."

Curt looked north, and took one step that way…but he did it slowly, as though unconcerned.

The older of the ladies, who had been quiet, was suddenly beside Curt, and she was yelling in her language and jabbing her finger through the air near him.

Curt stepped away from her, and forcefully pushed aside her hand...which made her stumble and fall to one knee. That's when Curt looked past the Nepalis and saw him. It was a glance, but there was no mistaking the recognition.

The two ladies followed Curt thirty feet or so to the next bend, loudly scolding him as they went. Now they were talking among themselves as they looked in the direction of his departure.

Oliver got to the bend with the Sherpa man...who then looked into his eyes. "He is a friend?"

"No! He is not a friend."

"You will watch him?" the man asked. "When the army comes, you can tell them where he is." Then he put out his hand to Oliver. "Will you help me with the father's pack?"

Returning to the pack, Oliver picked it up so his friend could get the straps of it around his shoulders. Molly arrived and handed the man the stout staff. And one of the ladies took his smaller pack.

After they said "Goodbye" to the Nepalis, Oliver stepped quickly ahead.

"Wait, Oliver!"

He turned. "Molly...I need to get on with this!"

Now looking back along the trail, he saw Bush and Marlaine. They were near. And Greg Barton was at the far bend. So he figured Curt had seen the first two.

He rushed ahead on the trail, but with changed expectations. When he rounded the next bend and saw Curt four hundred feet away, and running, he was not surprised. The man was now atop a small climb, and only glanced over his shoulder before moving from sight.

"Is he waiting?" Molly yelled.

He waited for her.

"No. He's running. And now he's out of sight."

Bush shouted "What's new?"

Marlaine asked "What did Curt do? Those people back there had tears in their eyes."

Molly opened her mouth as though to answer, then looked back along the trail. She sighed. "That would be terrible, wouldn't it, Oliver…even for a murderer. Do you think he knew the boy would die?"

Oliver said, to Bush and Marlaine, "Did you see the boy get hit?"

Greg Barton arrived before an answer came, and Marlaine spoke to him. "There was a landslide, and a boy got killed. Curt and the boy were hiding together."

"No!" said Molly. "Curt was hiding…against that boulder." She pointed. "The big one. The boy was kneeling in the open, only a couple feet away. And Curt could have reached out his hand…to help him."

Bush said. "The son of a bitch!"

Marlaine shook her head. "The man is a bastard!"

"Agreed," said Greg Barton. "But…crazy or not…I wonder if he's suffering…at all…for what he didn't do?"

Norm had arrived. "Shit!" does that matter? Will you ask him before you throw him off a fucking cliff?"

CHAPTER SIXTEEN

As Oliver entered Lobuche, it looked the same to him as it did three years earlier. It was a bowl-like three hundred feet, from which the trail departed northeast. Most of the handful of buildings were to the left of the trail, above it a few feet. To the right, and lower, were tents in an open space. Beyond the tents a stream ran through, mostly frozen.

There were men standing beside the tents. Now one of them said "I know him. I've seen him in Concord." So, Oliver knew he referred to New Hampshire. Then the man said "Perhaps we can get trekkers to help us."

Probably this meant the porters were striking. He remembered that, last time, the trail moving down onto Khumbu Glacier was in poor condition…being muddy and slippery…and there was a strike then.

He went to the buildings, intending to stay at the second or third one, where he had been before. But…standing in the doorway to the first was a young Sherpani, waving to him.

"You will please stop!" she said. "Come! Have tea!"

She seemed demanding, and not friendly."

Now she smiled and bowed. "Ek minett. Ek cup chiya, dinos."

He stopped. "Maybe I'll have one cup," he said, swinging his pack to a bench.

He went inside with, and toward a small kitchen area, to his right. And to do this, he stepped down a couple feet.

There were two tables and, along the hillside wall, a bench. From a rock fireplace, the cooking stove extended. Tending the fire was a mid-age Sherpani, who the young one went to.

On the bench sat four Nepali men, probably porters. Alone at one of the tables was Curt.

After Oliver stepped down, he stopped...because almost everyone was staring at him.

Curt was eating. And now...although he continued to look at his food...he said, "Yes...he's the one who let the child die. He only needed to pull the boy to himself. I don't want him here! Please tell him to get out!"

The younger lady raised a large wooden spoon and, shouting in her language, came toward Oliver. Now she pointed it at the door. "Get out! You're bad!"

Oliver thought about saying "Let's settle this! Step outside!" But he didn't. He figured Curt would laugh at that.

A porter got up and raised a fist toward him.

Oliver said, as he began to turn away, "Get to the end, Curt!"

Curt said, in a high voice, "Get to the end, Curt!"

Outside, Oliver got his pack and walked to the third building. He carried the pack in with him and set it inside, near the door. There was a mid-age Sherpani here, as well, and two young western men at a table.

This place was the same as the other, in that he would need to step down and to the right. Against that wall, the north one, was a rock fireplace, and a stove extending from it. The only difference was this kitchen room was larger, being about twenty feet across, and on the other side of that fireplace wall was the dormitory in which he had spent several nights.

"Namaste!" he said to the lady. "Could I have lemon tea, please!"

He nodded to the men, but they didn't respond. He sat at a table.

After the lady brought a cup to him and poured steaming water, he said "Do you have room in your dormitory for me?"

"Yes," she said, smiling. "I remember you!"

He said "Thanks…it's nice to see you. I have five friends coming…in a half hour."

"They can stay here. I have room."

Pointing to the men, he said "Did you cook more of that? Is it rice with chicken?"

"Yes. I'll make you a plate. I have rice cooked." And she turned away.

The two men spoke loudly as they ate, with one appearing to be at least temporarily dominant. A foot taller, and having a beard which reached nearly to the table, his loudness was in full sentences, while the smaller man usually only grunted. A couple times he tried to speak, and his words were cut off, rudely, by the other.

"Have you been to Everest base camp?" Oliver asked.

The big man answered without looking at him. "Yes. We surely have!" Then he continued to speak to his friend.

Oliver saw a bit of smoke come, puffing, from the side of the stove, near him. He said to the lady "It's getting breezy out. Windy."

The smaller man said "Put out the cigarette! I don't want any of our crap in my lungs!"

The Sherpa lady spoke angrily, and pointed at the stove. Then she got a stick and poked the end of it into the fire, in an effort to make it burn hotter.

The young Sherpani from the other building now appeared in the doorway. She pointed her spoon at Oliver and said, loudly, "He's bad!"

Then Curt was beside her and he, too, was pointing, with his arm above her shoulder.

"There he is!" said Curt. "There was an avalanche, just down the trail…and he could have saved the child…a little boy. Yes…that man! He was hiding behind a boulder…and he could have reached out and pulled the child to safety. But I saw him smile. He was smiling as the rock hit the boy's head; and his eyes were wide, as though he was enjoying watching it happen. I saw him! Then he knocked down a Nepali woman…as he escaped."

The Sherpani, who was yet at the stove, didn't look away from it during the story. She continued cooking, by stirring rice as it fried.

Oliver watched her, aware that the boy and his family had been in this town before their encounter with the avalanche. And now he saw a tear roll down her cheek.

Curt added "A Sherpa guide has gone to Pheriche to alert the army. So...this man will be thrown out of Nepal. And good riddance to him!"

The smaller of the two men said, to Oliver, "Go eat somewhere else!...or "I'll kick your ass!"

The big man said "You knocked down a Sherpa lady? I wonder if you could knock me down." And, putting the end of his beard inside his jacket, he stood up.

The Sherpa lady spoke angrily, In Nepali, to the girl in the doorway, then said "Go!" And after the girl was gone, she added, as she stirred the rice. "You sit! The army is here! We'll wait for him to come!"

But the bearded man stepped toward Oliver.

Curt came near. "Get the bastard!"

The Sherpa lady held up her spoon, and her other hand, as though to create a barrier. But it was Curt who suddenly intervened.

As the man stepped, Curt kicked the foot of his extended leg, knocking him off balance, and sending him to the floor.

Probably this man was not accustomed to being knocked down. He leaped to his feet and, raising his head, bellowed. But he would have been wiser to not raise his head and bellow, because that's when Curt kicked him between the legs. And he stopped bellowing, although his mouth was yet open as he went straight down.

Oliver got up.

Now the army man arrived, dressed in a Royal Nepalese Army uniform. As he stepped into the room, the only movement in it was that of the bearded am, who was yet down and trying to get back onto his chair.

Oliver sat.

The lady went to her pan and began to stir the rice as she spoke to the army man.

The man was a sergeant, and neatly dressed, with his pants inside his boots, bloused over the top edge of them. He was not a tall man, but apparently confident that he didn't need to be. To Oliver, he seemed to be at ease, and he had an honest face.

From the edge of the stairway, he looked down at Oliver.

The Sherpa lady also looked at him, and nodded toward the sergeant. She said "This man is a Gurkha, and with the Nepal Everest Expedition."

Curt, who hadn't moved, was beside the sergeant, although a bit nearer to Oliver. And he, too, was looking, his top lip raised slightly, showing his teeth.

"Excuse me!" said the sergeant to Curt. "Please step aside!...and sit there." He pointed to the table between Oliver and the two men, it being the only other one in the kitchen. Curt went to it and sat.

The sergeant spoke to Oliver. "A child has died, and there was a man who could have saved him. Was it you? Did you do this?"

"No! He did!" He pointed at Curt.

The sergeant looked at Curt, and then at a point halfway to Oliver. "Are you sorry the child died?"

Oliver sighed. "The boy was standing before him, and kneeled to get a better look. Then he took off his little hat and cleared the hair from his eyes."

He could feel his mouth tremble at that thought, and wondered if he, too, would have a tear.

Curt said "I saw this man move his arm toward the boy, in anger…as though to say "Get out!" That's why he didn't pull him in…not because he didn't think of it, but because he didn't want to. Didn't want his world cluttered…didn't want to be bothered." Curt held back his head and looked at the ceiling, then again at Oliver. "I saw him smile when the boy was hit…and his eyes were filled with pleasure. He enjoyed it!"

The sergeant said to Curt "Why were you looking at this man…as the rocks fell? Why did you study him, as the boy was hit?"

Curt didn't answer.

"You already knew he was a bad man?"

"Yes," said Curt, raising his hand toward Oliver. And it seemed he was about to say more, but the sergeant stopped him.

"Wait!" he said. Then he spoke to Oliver. "This is anger and sadness. The man who did it ought to be put out of Nepal. Mr…"

"Faulkner. My name is Oliver Faulkner."

"Oliver…the sergeant began,"…should an arrest be made, with handcuffs?" He turned to Curt. "Both of you, please, trekking permit and passport."

Molly came through the door, and paused there, surveying the scene; and then the others appeared behind her, Greg Barton being the closest to her.

"Oliver, what happened?" said Molly, as she moved forward, and came down the steps. "Has Curt been arrested?"

The sergeant said "This is Curt?" He glanced at the man and at the permits and passport, and dropped them onto the table. Then he turned to Molly. "Please tell what happened."

Curt yelled "My money has been stolen. By her!" He pointed to Marlaine, whose face was barely visible, between Bush and Norm.

"Did you steal his money?" the sergeant asked.

"Yes!" said Marlaine.

"She's my sister," Molly said. "She steals things, but gives them back. I…often return what she takes."

"Who has the money?" asked the sergeant.

Oliver said "I do." And after a pause, he added "It's a large amount, so Molly asked me to hold it."

"Will you return it to him?"

"This man is in Nepal because he was hired to kill me. That's what the money is."

Oliver wondered if that information would get himself kicked out. He was tied to whatever Curt did.

The sergeant went to the stove and asked the lady for tea, and she poured some. He blew across the cup and sipped from it, and looked toward the fire. He spoke in Nepali to the lady, and she answered him; but they did it lowly, and rapidly, and the only words he caught were "Orsho" and "Ang Babbhu".

He returned to Oliver, but when he spoke…it was to everyone. "How did you meet?" Then he looked at Greg Barton. "Sir…tell me how those people know each other, and why they are together, please." He bowed, slightly.

Greg said "I was in Namche when they came. Oliver first, then Norm and Marlaine and Bush." He pointed. "They sat and looked through the window at your world. Then Molly came. Then love came." He smiled. "Oliver and Molly fell in love."

Curt cut in, "Also, I came. Then they stole from me… and ran away. But I've caught them"

"Please!" The sergeant was waving his hand toward Curt, but not looking at him. "Mr…"

"Barton."

"What happened next?"

"They decided to climb a mountain…one that is a day or two west of Kala Patar. Then they included him." He indicated Curt. "He was asked to join…to help pay Oliver for guiding them."

"You say "They"…Mr. Barton. As though you are above."

After some silence, Oliver said "He's a guest…who can be with us, or not. But in Tukla he said he would come."

"Then…an honored guest," said the sergeant. "Is Oliver Faulkner the leader?"

"Yes."

"Then…why was this man, Curt, well ahead? Did he run away?" The sergeant turned to Oliver. Did he go ahead…in order to follow?"

Oliver said "Yes."

Curt snapped at the sergeant "You think Oliver Faulkner is good…because he looks it in his face? And because his friends are saying he is? We're all capable of murder."

"No!" said the sergeant. "We're all capable of killing. Only one of us is insane…and not a little crazy the way we all can be." He turned toward the Sherpa lady. But he was looking at his cup on the stove. She brought it to him and he drank from it. Then he said "We need to see what happened when the child died. Who will speak?"

Molly said "Oliver and I were a hundred feet or so from the boulder. We saw the boy get hit. But I couldn't see what was in Curt's face."

"We saw the rock hit the boy," said Marlaine. "Bush and I. But from farther away."

"So did I," said Norm.

Marlaine went on. "We could see Molly and Oliver nearer to us, and there was a man and a child at the boulder. And some people north of it."

Bush said You could see that it was a child kneeling by the rock...and the person hiding at it was a man."

The sergeant said "Mr. Barton. You didn't see?"

Greg Barton looked at the sergeant, as several seconds passed. He pursed the corners of his mouth and shook his head. "Sergeant, if this man, Curt, told you about what happened, how did he describe Oliver?"

"That he waved in anger at the boy...as though to push him away. And when he saw the boy get hit, he smiled."

Greg Barton said "Then...Curt saw Curt. And now I've seen him, too."

Molly said "My husband's friend, Ang Bubbha...went down the trail with the father's heavy pack."

Bush said "He told us what happened. He said the tall, blond man let the boy die."

"Ang Babbhu," said the sergeant, correcting Molly. Then he looked at Curt. "You must be to Namche in three days. Today is Monday...Sombar...you will be there Thursday.

You are not under arrest, but if you don't do this, you will be found and handcuffed. The men in Namche will escort you to Kathmandu."

Norm said "They don't have Gurkhas anymore?" Then he added "But maybe the sergeant has a radio in his tent."

"Mr. Monahan…do you have money?"

Curt seemed to be studying the palms of his hands., as they were before him on the table. He said, calmly, "I have none."

"I only took half his money," Marlaine said.

The sergeant continued to speak to Curt. "Mr. Faulkner can give you money for hotels and food." Then he asked, of Oliver, "How much would that be?"

Oliver stood and reached into his pocket. "Five hundred dollars. He has a plane ticket." He gave the money to Curt, by dropping it onto the table.

"He's got money…the lying bastard!" said Norm. "You don't need to give him any!"

The sergeant ignored Norm. "And you can give money to the family of the child?"

"Yes…whatever you think is right. But…I would like to give forty thousand rupiyaa. About eight hundred dollars."

"Why, Oliver?" Molly asked. "Why that amount?"

"It's how much my friend Sanu needs." He looked at the sergeant, "I speak of my friend in Kathmandu. He sells the instrument of the Gaini. If he works hard for a thousand years…he can save that much, and return to his village to build a house."

"That amount will do," said the sergeant.

Oliver counted it out, and held it forward.

"You can give the money to her." The sergeant was indicating the Sherpa lady. "Of the boy's mother, she is the sister...and she will go to Orsho tomorrow, in the morning."

The sergeant spoke to Curt. "You have eaten?"

"Yes...he ate!" said the Sherpa lady. Next door."

"Get your pack!" the sergeant ordered. He looked at his watch. "And get out of Lobuche! You can be to Pheriche in a couple hours. Going down is much easier."

Curt was holding the money Oliver gave him, and was looking at it.

Those near the door stepped aside, and Molly came nearer to Oliver and leaned against him.

Curt got up. After putting the money into his pocket, he deeply yawned and, holding his arms above his head, stretched. Then he smiled, and didn't look at anyone in the room, as he quickly departed.

The Sherpa lady asked them to decide menus for dinner and breakfast, so they did that.

"And so...that's the end of Curt?" asked Marlaine.

"What a relief."

Bush laughed. "Where's to hide...out there? I mean, up there."

"That would be insane," Molly said. "Aren't you glad he's gone, Oliver?"

Norm said "Maybe we can get on with our lives...as they ought to be lived."

Outside, they went to the north end of the building, to the dormitory door...and entered. Oliver told them to sleep on bunks away from the stove wall.

"Why?" asked Bush, turning away from it.

Oliver said "Tonight...the striking porters will be in the kitchen, talking and drinking beer. The night will be cold, and they'll crank up the fire, and linger by it until it's almost out. Most of that end of the building, particularly the top bunks, will be in thick smoke...in the early hours."

Norm said "But you'd have to be stupid not to be aware of it...and move away."

"The smoke arrives late," said Oliver. "Into a dark world, in which a person is breathing deeply in an effort to get used to the thinner air. The woody smell of a fire has been heavy for hours. In the dark. So...you don't know of the change. Your heart begins to jump...to do a flip, now and then...as you fight for air, and for sleep. But blaming it on altitude, you breathe more deeply...in the dark. And you wonder, as though from a distant place, if maybe you ought to dress and go down the trail. Then...someone turns on a light, and you see the smoke."

"Ah!...no one is that stupid!" said Norm.

"Dammit!" said Oliver. "I was!"

They all got into their bags and napped.

Before dinner, as it was near to darkness, four other travelers came in and went to the kitchen wall; so Oliver warned them about the smoke. Then he decided to speak to his friends.

"Is everyone awake?"

In the dim light he saw Bush and Marlaine and Norm move their heads. Greg Barton said "Yes."

Molly rubbed against him.

He began. "It seems that you've dismissed Curt.

And...even considering the angry words between Norm and I...there is an uplifted difference in your attitudes. A livelier step was there as we entered this dorm, and then you snored in a relaxed way...as though you've let something go. But...it's my duty to tell you that Curt is not gone."

"But he is!" said Marlaine. "The sergeant went outside and watched him walk down the trail. Surely he wouldn't come back."

"Now that he's known here...where would he eat?" said Norm.

Oliver said "I'm going west of Kala Patar. Maybe all of you ought to go east of it."

"So you can be alone out there?" said Bush.

Norm said "He's gone! I'm going west of Kala Patar."

Everyone was quiet for awhile. Then Greg Barton said "Whatever Curt wants to kill in you, is in himself. It could be that he's not sure what it is."

Molly said "A blind hate?"

Greg Barton said "But everything that hates...loves, or once did."

"And so..." Oliver began. "You think...maybe Curt is striking out at what he hates, but it's hidden in the cloudiness."

"That's where the worst part of the human mind is," said Greg Barton. "In the cloud...far from the center. When we strike out blindly at another human...the cause can be hate or love."

Molly said "Then isn't it obvious that Curt held Oliver in an elevated place...before he met him? He didn't kill Oliver that first day, in Namche, and it would have been easy to do, in the dark. So...he isn't here for the money, but also he lingers over this desire...not because he hates the handsomeness, intelligence, and character of Oliver. Isn't it a personal thing, in that it involves both of them?"

Greg Barton said "Another's character can become elevated to the personal…inside the murderer. The handsomest, brightest, most kind and courteous, can be "just there"…as the murderer's possession. But it's out of reach. The "just there"…is beyond the mist."

"It's there…but not there?" said Molly.

"It's why some kill presidents;…they're at the top. And the concept "the top"…is inside the killer…being what they hate or love…or both."

Molly said "Whatever is in Oliver…in particular…is in himself. He's seeing it clearly, but through the mist."

"Let's not elevate Curt, too much," said Oliver. "Our view of his actions depends on the "just there" part.

"I agree," said Greg Barton. "But we think he'll be back. So…we see his hate as being a powerful one. How could it be that?...unless that which was driven into the mist was strong love twisted, and beaten."

"What should I make of hate based on twisted love?" said Oliver. "Other than to recognize it as powerful…if that's the cause. But…I don't know what Curt has inside. Won't my concern about that…have more sincerity after he's dead?"

"Sure!" said Greg Barton. "Sorry, Oliver!"

Molly said "Greg knows you'll defend yourself. Isn't it true…that you never have been afraid of Curt?"

"When I step into the ring with Curt…I'll drop him six feet. Would you have me think otherwise? But, Molly…my hair might be standing on end. How could anyone not fear hate that strong? Dammit…I need to destroy whatever is in his head."

"Yeh…well…" Greg Barton began, "I'm going with you, Oliver. It's my choice."

"And it's mine!" said Molly.

There was silence for a minute.

Molly said "I don't like being theoretical about a murderer. How do you see a person's soul?…Curt's, or mine, or anyone's?"

Oliver raised his shoulders, "A person's unguarded actions often show the tenor of it. You can sense an unobstructed path when you see a tear rolling down a cheek. Yes…dear Sherpa lady…I saw it! Did you see it, Molly? And yet she attended to us. There it is! But…what of a soul that's not all there? You're right, Molly. Maybe we can't get at Curt."

In the kitchen they sat at the table Oliver had, earlier. The lady brought two more chairs; and he and Molly, Greg Barton, and Marlaine were at the table, with Norm and Bush at the next, but almost touching.

Six porters were along the west wall, on the bench, and the newly arrived travelers were at the table once occupied by the bearded man and his friend. The center table, where Curt sat, was empty.

The lady, with two younger female helpers, had most menus ready, the main part being rice and chicken. Also, the Sherpa stew was ready, with potatoes, onions, carrots, and green peppers. And she could make chapatti…a thin, pan-bread, and she had eggs.

After they ate, Greg Barton said "let's have a bottle of beer. Oliver…? It's your decision."

Molly said "Look how big the bottles are." She pointed toward the porters. "I would only want a glassful."

Oliver said "Good idea! Molly and I will share one. Let's get only a few bottles…so we can avoid a late start in the morning."

So they ordered beer, and…in a bit…were sipping on it.

Oliver asked "Greg what color was your wife's hair?"

"Very light brown. Almost blond. Nearly the same shade as Molly's. And of Bush's parka."

Oliver went on. "Greg…when you were in Namche you had a red parka, and now you've got a dark brown one. How do you explain that?"

"It suddenly came upon me to buy it," said Greg, looking down at it, then touching it. He sighed. "My wife had a dark brown parka…and sometimes her long hair would be on it. Before she zipped it, she'd tuck the hair in behind her…but it would come out later and be in her face. Then I'd nestle my face against hers."

Bush said "Oliver, how do you explain that you and Molly have dark blue parkas?"

"I feel more at ease in a dark color," said Oliver. "It suits me."

"It does," said Marlaine. "Very much."

"Speak for your own!" said Molly. "Do you prefer tan or black?" She was referring, probably, to Bush and Norm. "As for me…" She leaned against Oliver. "I've been told…my husband sees me naked…every time I tuck in my strawberry blond hair."

"It's brown!" Marlaine said.

"Well…yours isn't black!" said Molly. "Now that we're onto the truth. Your hair doesn't match Norm's parka…only the dye does."

There was silence.

Molly said "I'm being a bitch. Don't anyone try to stop me!"

Silence again.

"My hair is brown," said Marlaine. "A frizzy, bird's nest brown. My lips are thin. My skin is flat white. Shall I steal your pearly teeth, little sister bitch?"

Silence. Then Marlaine laughed. And Molly laughed.

Bush said "I like your eyes, Marlaine."

Silence. Then everyone laughed.

"And so," Greg Barton said, "You wear a black, mock-turtleneck sweater...Oliver...about every son of a bitchin' day. I'm sick of it! Do you think you're captain of a submarine?"

"Well...Mr. superior ass..." said Oliver. "Why don't you acknowledge that you're a subspecies...that I'm captain of."

Norm said "You should hear yourselves! I'm ashamed to be part of this."

"Well at least you got that far," said Oliver.

Molly said "Are you finished, Oliver?"

"With what?"

"I don't know! But...we should do it more often."

Everyone laughed.

"Yes!" said Molly. "Also...did you know that when you kiss me roughly...and tear my lip apart...and I say "Ahh!"... it doesn't mean I like it, do it again!"

"But you said "Don't stop!"..."

"I said "Don't!...stop!"

He laughed. "Sorry!...your lips are my treasure. Did you know...when you were asleep, in Tyangboche, your mouth was wide open and you snored so loudly that the girl in the kitchen, downstairs, said "I think it's raining out this morning!" I heard her shout it to her mother."

Bush said "How come nobody attacks me? I'm not good enough?"

"We don't have the time, Bush," said Greg Barton. "Anyway…you do it to yourself every few minutes."

"Do what to myself?"

After a bit of silence, Marlaine said "Doesn't that stunt your growth? But look how big he is!"

"Who?" asked Bush.

Oliver laughed. Molly did…then she said "Nepalis are little. Should they do more of it?"

"No!" said Oliver. "They should eat more!"

Norm said "It's good to be little!"

Bush said "I'm big…and I guess there's nothing I can do about it."

"What's done is done," said Greg Barton, sighing, then laughing. "And here we are."

CHAPTER SEVENTEEN

In the morning, when they departed Lobuche, snow was falling in large flakes. And because a half hour later it was yet doing that, with addition of a breeze, Norm and Bush and Marlaine wanted to turn back.

Oliver said "I think this will stop soon."

Then wind gusted through.

"The wind's coming up," said Norm. "It'll be getting worse."

"I wouldn't blame you if you go back," Oliver shouted. "I'll wait for you in Gorak Shep."

Norm said "Maybe I want you to say…you can be wrong."

"I can be wrong!" said Oliver. "This storm might last. But I'm going ahead."

The storm soon passed. At Gorak Shep they stopped to buy tea from a couple transient, raggedly dressed Nepalis, squatting in a floorless building.

Greg Barton said "Make sure the water boils each time they fill the kettle. But this is the last place. From now on we'll melt snow…and boil our own."

"Oliver…"Molly leaned against him. "Did I snore last night?"

He put his arm around her. "I didn't notice."

"I think I don't do it very often. But it bothers you?"

"No! When I heard you snoring in Tyangboche…I thought it was cute."

Norm said, to Marlaine, "Now that you mention it, Molly's lips are fuller than yours."

Oliver said "Is that meant to be praise…or insult?"

Norm had been looking at Marlaine when he spoke. Now he looked at the ground, and then at his cup of tea.

At the foot of Kala Patar they stopped and looked around.

Norm said to Oliver, "You were right about the storm passing. Thanks for not rubbing my nose in the error."

"I think you didn't make an error, Norm. Neither of us knew what the storm would do. But I know the trail. For you it was perhaps like moving onto a wild sea…and it was correct for you to hesitate."

Molly said "Aren't you more likely than Norm…to go ahead? No offense, Norm. My husband likes to stretch the bounds of safety."

Oliver said "I often go forward into difficulty. If you're careful in the mud, it's sometimes the shortest way to the picnic. But…less arrogantly…I'd like to point out that Norm chose to be at sixteen thousand feet in the Himalayas."

Marlaine came near. "What's this about a picnic?"

"Is that the way we're going?" asked Bush, pointing west. "This hill that we're near...is it Kala Patar?"

That's just south of Pumo Ri, you said. So...it's east, that way, to Everest base camp. But we're heading the other way." Again he indicated west.

Norm said "But...Ri is another word for mountain. You know that, of course."

Bush yelled "Why am I being ignored?"

"Yes, Bush, that way!" said Oliver. "There's the southern tip of Changri Shar Glacier., which we need to cross. And it looks passable, from here...in spite of the many rocks on it."

Molly said "Such a beautiful morning! The sky is deep blue...the mountains are golden."

"I'd like to live in Nepal," said Marlaine.

"I would, too!" Bush said.

"Sure!" Norm snapped. "And in three weeks you'd be crying for a shower, and soft toilet paper...and a telephone so you could order pizza."

"Maybe," said Marlaine, quietly.

Norm said "You'd miss the world."

"But maybe not," Marlaine said. "I don't miss the news of it. Or those other things either...except a shower. I...could learn to use a bucket of water."

"So could I!" said Bush.

Through the rocks was a trail on Changri Shar, heading west. It consisted of an occasional pile of small rocks placed on a large one.

The glacier was firm, with a bit of powdery snow.

In awhile…at the far side of Changri Shar, at the southern tip of land, they saw two small, stone buildings.

Molly spoke to Oliver. "Do they bring cattle this far north, in the summer? Oh…this is what you called a Kharka."

Oliver said "When I was little we called poop, Kaka. And so…" he looked down at his left foot as it hit the ground. "Kaka." Then he looked at his right foot. "Kharka. Well…kaka…kharka."

Molly stepped ahead. "Kaka…Oliver…kaka…Oliver. Yes, why not poop on him when he asks for it?"

Greg Barton said "I've heard enough!" he looked upward. "Don't mind them, Johanna…we did it, too. We were often silly."

At the base of the tip of land, which climbed quickly away, they stopped to rest.

Oliver said "Please have water…even if you're not thirsty. And a biscuit or candy bar, or something."

As Marlaine was trying to take off her pack, she asked Norm for help. Norm was the nearest man to her, but Oliver wondered if there was a different reason for the choice. And Norm was quick to help her…without a word, and as though he wanted to.

"I broke my sunglasses," she said. "Ahh, damn!"

After her pack was down she retrieved her glasses from the snow. He could see that one handle was separated.

She asked Norm, "Do you have spare sunglasses?"

"Yes!" Norm snorted. Then he turned away and, reaching down to his pack, brought out a candy bar. He unwrapped it, and took a bite from it. "You'd better return to

Lobuche!" But he didn't look at her as he spoke. Then he got out a water bottle and, stepping ten feet or so from the trail, stood drinking and eating as he looked westward.

Greg Barton had walked about a hundred feet southward, onto Changri Nup, and in the jumble of rocks of all sizes, some atop others, only his upper body was showing.

Marlaine stepped closer to Bush, and spoke in a low tone. "I broke my sunglasses, Bush. Do you have extra ones?"

Bush said "Yes. I think they're here…in this side pocket." He began to search. Then he handed them to her.

"Thank you for the kindness, Bush." And as she leaned down to her pack, "It comes easily to you."

Molly whispered to Oliver. "What are you thinking? That Norm came to the bridge…and turned away?"

"Apparently."

She said "A mountain bridge…swaying in a wind, with holes in it and missing boards…far above the raging water. And yet, there it was? Oliver, did we see Norm…retreat into the mist?"

When Greg Barton returned, Oliver spoke quietly to him. "Did you look for tracks?"

"Yes. I didn't see any."

"Have you had water, Greg? Rest for a minute."

"I already did, Oliver. I'm ready to go."

Molly said "Norm has gone ahead. Look!…he's two hundred feet away…or more."

Norm was moving in what seemed a casual way, looking at and above his immediate surroundings, which showed as mostly snow and ice, with rocks. Now he looked back, and waved.

Oliver said "I think it's about half a mile to where this edge turns. I hope he waits for us there, because we might head northwest instead of west...at the bend. Also...he ought to be thinking a bit about Curt."

"Wouldn't we have seen Curt's tracks?" asked Molly.

"A person doesn't need to get near Kala Patar before turning west," Oliver said. "He could do it earlier, and get to where Norm is."

As they prepared to go ahead, Oliver saw Bush miss a step. He had been standing nearby, before beginning to cross a five feet wide space between himself and his gear. On the way to the gear was a rock about eight inches high and a foot square, which he obviously intended to step onto, but when he got to the very edge of it he stumbled. After that he put on his pack...easily, but slowly.

"Molly...take the lead, sweetheart. It's a couple minutes to where we last saw Norm. Marlaine and Bush, you can follow her." He went to Greg and touched his shoulder. They both watched the others move away.

"What's wrong? Is it Bush? I saw him stumble."

'if he's off badly, we'll need to spot it," said Oliver. "It's now just a bit after noon, a safe time for getting him back to Lobuche before dark."

They went ahead. At the area where Norm was when he waved, and only a hundred feet or so from the bend, there was no indication that Bush was seriously off. Perhaps he wasn't off to any extent, because he didn't stumble again.

Oliver saw Molly look back, apparently wanting him to attend...so he went to the front.

"What is it?"

"Nothing, Oliver! I just want you with me."

He said "Let's continue to the bend. We'll move around it, northwest, about half a mile, and look things over. So, do you see Norm's tracks?" He put his arm around her shoulders, and looked at the snow ahead.

He heard a whistle from behind. When he turned, he saw Greg Barton pointing at Bush, who had stepped from the trail and was standing, unmoving, staring at the ground. And Greg was holding Bush's hat. Evidently…Bush wasn't aware of having lost it.

He went to Bush and touched his shoulder.

"How do you feel?"

Bush looked at him. "Oh…fine."

"Where's your hat?"

Bush looked blankly at him, and scratched his cheek.

Greg gave him his hat.

"I'm sending you down, Bush," said Oliver. "To Gorak Shep…or maybe Lobuche. You can come back in a day or two. Marlaine…will you take him?"

"Yes. But am I strong enough? All the way to Lobuche?"

"It's nearly one o'clock," Oliver said. "I'll walk a few hundred feet with you…then you can guide him to Gorak Shep. If by three or four he's still off…go to Lobuche. But I think you won't need to do that." He spoke to Greg Barton. "Greg… when you get to the bend go northwest a half mile…then across the north-running glacier, due west, to the other promontory, and wait for me."

"No! I…" Greg hesitated. "Oliver…when I come to the north-running glacier, I might move onto it only part of the way. Is that all right?"

"Yeh, sure. I'll be back in a half hour."

"I remember from the map," said Molly. We could walk up the middle of the glacier…maybe…straight north, and get to Changri La that way. It's mainly scree."

Greg Barton said "But it shows on the map as a deep valley. Johanna and I will look at it, Oliver. Probably, we'll be just beyond it, when you get back."

"You said Johanna…but, you and Molly will be waiting for me. Right?"

"Yes. Sorry!"

It was four o'clock when he returned to where he departed from them. Then…looking along the edge of the glacier as it ran northwest, he didn't see them on that stretch, but their tracks were clearly showing, and he was happy to see three sets.

After another twenty minutes passed he came to the north-running part, and looked westward toward the other promontory. There were a couple tents set up, near the middle of the glacier.

He walked onward, and when he got to the middle, Greg and Molly were a couple hundred feet ahead, waving at him. Now looking north, he thought Greg was correct in assuming it would be difficult to get out of that valley a quarter of a mile into it, and be much higher, where you'd need to turn west to Changri La. Too much deep snow, maybe.

He moved on. Then he noticed there were only two sets of tracks. So…he returned to where he had been looking up the middle. There, he found that the other set headed almost directly south, out across Changri Nup. He got out his binoculars, but could see no movement in that direction.

He dropped to his knees and examined the tracks. They didn't belong to Norm or anyone in his group. He figured it was Curt.

When he got to the others, Molly asked about Bush and Marlaine.

"Probably tomorrow they'll be back up. But I sent them to Lobuche. Did you see the tracks heading south?"

"Yes, and we felt angry at Norm," said Molly, "when we saw the tracks. Why would he go that way? Or, maybe he's getting confused. Think so?"

Greg Barton said "Below us…on the part of the glacier to the south of us is that line of mountains which run west from Lobuche…until they curve north and join Changri La's moutains. Do you suppose he's decided to climb Lobuche west, alone?"

Oliver sighed. "Molly…remember that sign on the wood post, south of Pheriche? And we saw the foot-prints in the freshly overturned dirt?" He looked at Greg Barton. "The tracks are Curt's."

Molly said "Oh, my God! Then…what about Norm? Do you think Curt did something to him?"

He said "We need to find out, by walking back along the trail. Repack the tents! Let's not get separated from our gear, or each other."

After again crossing the north-running glacier, they went along the edge of Changri Nup, and didn't speak until standing at the bend.

"This is almost to where Norm waved to us," said Molly. "Maybe he's all right. He just wandered away from the trail…in his self-serving way."

Oliver said "It's my fault! I should have ordered him to return to us, and stay near!"

"We all grew accustomed to him being contrary," said Greg Barton.

They went ahead another fifty feet.

He said "There!" and he pointed. "Some tracks are heading north, into the hill." He went to them and kneeled. "Two men...and one came back."

Greg Barton said "Oliver...this happened as we attended to Bush."

Oliver followed the tracks, but didn't need to walk far. About twenty feet from the main trail, Norm was in the snow...beyond a boulder. He was bareheaded, his hat several feet away, and he had been given a killing blow on the back of the head.

He got the hat and put it on Norm, and pulled up the hood. With his ice axe he began digging a shallow grave, and Greg Barton helped, with his axe.

"He didn't turn his head before being hit," said Oliver. His hat was on..see how it's torn? But there's no blood on it. It was an ineffective blow, probably from an ice axe."

"So..." Greg Barton began, "How do you explain that his skull is crushed...in that spot?"

"He was only dazed. Then, when he was down, and his head bare, Curt hit him again, in the same place." Oliver shuddered. He reached down and touched the body. "Ah!... screw the method of the madness! We're sorry you're dead, pal!"

Molly kneeled beside Norm, getting his wallet and passport. After opening the wallet, she said "Thanks for having my sister's picture, Norm But...why did you court a thief, and not let her steal your heart?"

They returned to where the tents had been set up, then walked beyond...all the way to the promontory which touched the line of mountains coming down from Changri La.

"There's about twenty minutes of light remaining," said Olive. "Let's walk along this as it heads north. The land will be touching our left hand, and I've seen no tracks from the south. We'll step upon the land, and climb it fifty feet or so...then stay at that height on it as it goes north."

When that amount of time passed, Molly said "Isn't it too dark, now, for Curt to see us? He must be to the south of the promontory. If we move farther up this, northward... let's also go down to the glacier. Wasn't it mostly scree down there, along the edge of it? This walking is too rough, with these big rocks. And there isn't any trail."

Oliver said "When it's light tomorrow we'll find a trail along this. But I want to stay up here, tonight.

"Greg Barton said "It'll be warmer up here, Molly. And that glacier bulges against this land, in some places. I...remember thinking, as I looked at the map, that it would be safer to be up high."

"See that flat place ahead?" said Oliver. We'll set up our tents here, now...and then after it gets very dark, we'll put them there. In case we're being seen."

They set the tents, pretending to be doing it for the night...and waited.

Molly said "Shall I give Norm's wallet and passport to the sergeant...or hand them over at the army post in Namche?"

"Wait until we get to Kathmandu, Molly. They'll contact his family."

Oliver, don't ever ship me from Nepal. It would cost too much…and be trouble. Do you think Norm believed in an afterlife?"

"I assume so…or else he would have told us he didn't. Other than his tendency, when seemingly hopeless, to say that God made it, then left it alone, he probably had a fundamental Jewish place. I wish we knew."

"He was wanting to love my sister…and she was waiting for him to try harder."

Greg Barton said "He most likely did. But he locked his self up…and so, her love didn't get into him far enough to draw it out. "Ah!...as you say, what do we know about Norm?"

Oliver said "It seemed, in Namche, that he emptied himself a bit. Maybe she was at the edge…then."

"And when she asked him for sunglasses? That ended it?" said Molly.

"He turned away," Oliver said. "And we'll never know why. It's sad he didn't know of the eternity in his final word to her."

"The night is very dark, Oliver," said Greg Barton. "Are you wanting to move?"

"Yes. Molly…grab the bottom of my pack as we walk, and I'll take us to that other place. Greg…you can hold the bottom of her."

"Mr. Barton…remember who I am…please!"

CHAPTER EIGHTEEN

In the morning the sky was dark blue, and the mountain's white...sun-fired. Oliver, awake before the others, remembered a western man sitting not far from Pangboche, at a place an hour along the trail to Gokyo, encountering much beauty saying, unhappily, "It's all the same!" and he seemed to be a bursting man. Oliver thought, now, that if the man stopped to live there...maybe he'd put aside his turbulence, and be a mirror to the sameness. And yet, Oliver now admitted, the human mind is uncomfortable with perfection...and needs to break off a piece of it...in order to fit into the neighborhood.

He roused the others, and told them, gently but firmly, to eat and drink.

"But you don't need to insist!" Molly said.

He looked at Greg Barton, who shrugged his shoulders and said "I came here to think less. Let me advise you, from my experience...to be quiet awhile."

In a minute, Molly said "Please eat! Or...die!"

He put powdered milk and dried oatmeal into his bowl, with hot water from some Molly had carried.

After eating…he set the bowl on a boulder, and used his binoculars to look north along the mountain range, mostly at the glacier's edge, then he looked down to where they had arrived at the promontory.

"What's ahead, Oliver?" Greg Barton asked.

Molly said "But, look for Curt! It's OK…I'm cranky, now. Tell him what's ahead, Oliver!" she laughed.

"Drink some tea, Molly. And eat! So…yes, I looked north. We can continue to walk somewhat above the glacier. Keep your eyes open for trail markers."

Greg Barton, and then Molly did. Now, when Greg moved closer to Oliver, so did she.

In a gentle tone, she said "The glacier is quite rounded, isn't it…also jumbly and holey. I see crevasses. Oliver…" Now she leaned against him. "That is such a huge body of snow. If we went up the middle of it, maybe we couldn't have climbed out. I mean…way up inside it."

"The way we're going looks safe," he said. "It might be half a mile up to the pass, and in that distance we ascend seven or eight hundred feet."

"It looks easy!" she said.

Oliver and Greg Barton spoke at the same time. "It won't be!"

As they ascended, the way was safe and steady, but painful and slow. The ground was packed snow and ice with rocks on it. For awhile mostly it was scree, but some were the size of a hand, and there were boulders. A half dozen times, Oliver saw what seemed to be trail markers, as small rocks were resting together on a big one as though placed there.

They got into a rhythm of moving twenty feet or so and then resting about half a minute.

Molly said "Three or four deep breaths…and I feel strong again."

Then it became steeper; and they went ahead ten feet or so before stopping and breathing deeply.

It was a slow journey. At eight o'clock, after a half hour of climbing, they were only a quarter of the way, and decided there was no need to rush. Why not have fifteen deep breaths at each rest? And why not enjoy the view?

For awhile they couldn't see much, below, over the glacier, but eventually got high enough to.

"Nice view!" said Greg Barton. And after another deep breath, he added "Would you believe I once climbed Pumo Ri?"

Molly pointed east. "Is it one of them?"

The range across the glacier was part of theirs, joining it above, and it began almost straight up from where Norm died. Just there, near where they found him, was what led up to a small peak of about twenty thousand feet, the first of four in a couple mile stretch, eastward, each one a bit higher.

"That range runs up to Chumbu," said Greg Barton. "Pumo Ri is beyond it, along the upper wall. I remember how much falling debris there was. My friend was injured. Ah…I was young then. And now I'm old."

"Don't be sad!" said Oliver. "You'll have new things to remember."

Molly said "What's sixty five to a stud? Every time we stop I breathe harder than you."

Greg pointed southeast. "There's Lobuche West. It's about twenty thousand. We're almost that high. What are we, nearly eighteen thousand?"

Oliver said "Aren't you glad you're here?"

He looked south, but knew Greg and Molly were studying him, perhaps to determine if he included both in the question.

Molly said "Other than the sadness of Norm's death, I'm happy to be here. And I might feel happier to be anywhere…after this. I mean…because of this happiness, I'll be happier in my life."

"Let's move on!" said Greg Barton.

"But…what about you?" asked Oliver.

"This is beautiful," said Greg. "Yes…I'm glad to be here. Although…something is missing…and it hurts, because the memory of it is strong here." And he began to step away, upward.

"You're a teacher, Mr. Barton!" said Molly. "You lived long enough to be wise. You can lead awhile, can't he, Oliver?"

"Yes. But…I didn't equate my leadership with being wise."

Greg Barton stopped and turned to them. "I've lived long enough to be old…or, rather, to feel old. But I think you're right about the teacher part…because you can learn as much from my mistakes as from what I do properly."

"Maybe we need you to tell us which is which," said Oliver.

"At this moment," said Greg, "I think that you two belong here…and everywhere, in this life. I belong here more than most other places."

"Why is that?" asked Oliver.

"It's easier here to feel the sameness between you and all reality." Greg said. "This a grand place, yet simple. Uncluttered. You can be unthinking before it. You can get outside yourself."

"Be as a mirror?" Oliver said.

Molly said "As before a clear sea?"

"Yes, Molly. Yes, Oliver. And so you know I'm not being critical of you...who stand in one mirror. As lovers... you belong everywhere you stand. I...sure! Once...Johanna and I were in the middle of a great boulevard in Paris, and were holding one another when the light changed and dozens of cars came thundering toward us. The wind followed them to us. Yes!...after they piled up into chaos, we felt a gentle breeze, and walked away. If I'm a teacher...there it is. There's your highest place. As lovers...being where you ought to be...is being anywhere you are."

Oliver said "The love you shared isn't gone. You have it. You need to go on living."

"I am," said Greg. "And this is where I want to be."

Oliver said "Here?...where you most feel what is missing? Where you can love the most, but be the saddest? You need to look for light...in your continuance."

Greg said "My sadness is a personal necessity. But, Oliver, the power in tragedy resides both in hope's light, and in the uncertainty...as one wonders about it. So, I don't cater to the tragic. I have to do with sadness only, because in this place there seems to be nothing between me and my memory. And yet, something is missing, and I'm glad of the sadness."

"And yet…this life stands between you and Johanna," said Oliver. "But…I think your life ought to run its proper course."

"It is!" said Greg Barton. "It does!"

As they neared the pass, the glacier was getting onto the rock, so they climbed well above it.

Oliver said "It appears that the trail will be going back down a bit toward the glacier before we get to the entrance. We need to go around steep rock…then straight in. I mean, up and in."

Molly said "What trail?"

Greg Barton laughed. "The one leading to where you want to go. Do you have a special island, Molly?"

"Yes…I'm here, Mr. Barton."

Oliver said "I didn't exactly see a trail. I've seen little rocks that were piled up…maybe long ago."

"Maybe the trail is on the glacier," said Molly.

After moving around the steep wall of rock, they entered an opening snowy and yet rock-strewn, with large boulders predominating at the northern edge.

When they went ahead to the center of the opening, and then up into it, the way appeared to be unobstructed between heights for more than five hundred feet.

Oliver said "Let's rest here." Then he looked at the glacier they were leaving. "We're high enough now to see the part we crossed…way down there. Is that someone walking? Halfway across. Can you see?"

Taking off their packs, they sat on them. Molly got out her binoculars, but was interested in what lay ahead.

"It's not much of a rise to the other side," she said. "And this snow seems firm. Why isn't it deeper?"

Greg Barton said "I've read that this area can be icy when you're climbing. In summer there's frequent melting and refreezing. And maybe there wasn't much snow here this winter. Although, there's quite a bit at those boulders over there. Maybe it slid down."

Oliver said "According to the chart it's about seven hundred feet across this pass…and not so rocky on the other side, but snowier. Let me see your binoculars, sweetheart."

He looked down to where the crossed Changri Nup, at the base of the north-running part, and found the person moving along. Now he could tell that the movement was into the middle of the glacier, northward. And, although the man had his hood up, on this sunny day, Oliver knew it was Curt.

Molly said, as she yet looked into the pass, "At the other end is deeper snow, Oliver? Yes, I remember the map. At the crest of this, it's open snow before we go down the other side."

"How do you feel, you two?" he asked.

Molly nodded and smiled.

"I'm comfortable," said Greg Barton. "Shake me on your way back. If I'm living…take me down." He smiled.

"Now tell me the truth," said Oliver.

Greg said "I feel fine. And the rise through the pass is not bad, apparently."

"Listen!" Oliver began, calmly and gently. "The man walking down there is Curt."

"That's not finished?" said Molly.

Oliver went on. "Whether or not he can ascend an hour or two and then get out of the valley…we don't know. He might've met someone who went that way, and was told he can do it. But…as for us…let's go! We'll move through the pass." He looked at his watch. "It's noon. By two or three o'clock…after we enjoy the place…I'll let both of you go down the other side and get well away."

"And then what?" Molly asked. "Oliver…do you need to be heroic? All we've got to do is stay a day ahead of him. You come with us…down the other side."

He put his arms around her "I'll wait here…later, when Curt arrives…he and I will get to what's been put off. And when you get away, Molly, be brave and strong…like Greg Barton."

For awhile they remained at the entrance, looking at the view…and agreeing many times that it was beautiful. Almost entirely so. It was too bad the range across the glacier obscured the sight of Pumo Ri. You could see some of Everest, Nuptse, and Lhotse. But the deepest snow was southward, at the jumble of mountains running far.

He walked to the north side of the entrance, and Molly and Greg followed.

They could see more clearly southward beyond the tip of Ama Dablam.

"It ties it all together," said Oliver. "To look back where you came."

Molly said "I can feel my whole life. Remember Namche, Oliver?…when we went above town, on the Thame trail, and looked down the valley. I think Christ did that, too. Where are you from, Mr. Barton?"

Greg didn't answer immediately. Removing his mitt, he rubbed his fingers across his chin. Then he said "Yes…he might have."

"Connecticut?" said Molly.

"Yes. But I don't feel the need to go back that far, unless a remembrance comes by itself into my head."

Oliver said "I wonder if John Finn made it safely back to Alaska? He was a tail gunner on B25s in World War Two. My father went through that as a submariner. And...my brother died early, last year."

Greg Barton said "I guess if we sat here long enough, Oliver, we'd get to all your points...and try to make sense of God's ethics." He sighed. "If you're compassionate inside... things are the same."

Oliver said "In that you love the bad as well as the good?"

"Yes. You've got to sigh yourself beyond man's actions... and accept reality."

"Even as you try to get rid of the bad," said Oliver.

"Sure!" said Greg.

"You've got to be firm in the compassion," said Oliver. "If the Japanese had their way, none of us would be here. But, my brother, who died early, would have died earlier, as a child...if we didn't use a fist to turn the other cheek."

Molly said "What we don't understand, we ought to love even as we're hating it? Is that compassion?"

"Sure!" said Oliver. "But...compassion demands that we have humility. Sometimes we need a fist. Always we need an open door to the truth. And, as to what humans cause...we apply justice to actions only."

"You're saying," began Greg, "that we should avoid unquestioned certainty about what's come to the door."

"Using a fist is an occasional necessity. Giving a cigarette before or after...is an action reaching deep into the human heart. Greg...when you were little, did you play baseball?"

"Yes…baseball and football. But when I was three, a woman came to our house and told my mother I broke her window, with a big rock. As my mother told the story, years later, she said "The rock was big…" and she held her hands about eight inches apart. And when we went to see the window it was six feet above the ground. The lady stood there, studying, and she was holding the rock…then she looked down at this little kid, me, three years old, and she shook her head and said "No!...he couldn't have done it!"

"But you did!" said Molly.

Oliver said "When I was two…my parents moved to Newport, Rhode Island…briefly…to a house with a heavy-wire fence in the backyard. I remember it. My mother said "We put you in the yard, and I said "He can't climb over that fence"…but the next time we looked out the window you were gone."

Molly said "I did these things, too."

They waited, but she was silent.

Oliver said "Molly you're an athlete with a questing heart, or you wouldn't be here."

She said "I threw a rock down the street…in my hometown. If you were there you wouldn't believe I could've thrown it that far. It went through Annie Friedman's window." She sighed. "I went to her…that day…and told her I did it."

"I can see you doing it," said Oliver, hugging her. "Yes. Both things."

Molly said "I heard a murderer, once…say he enjoyed being mean to animals when he was little. That's because I was just thinking about Curt."

Oliver sighed. "Maybe he wasn't. We don't know what kind of killer he is." He looked at Greg Barton. "Do I have to go that far...inside him?"

Greg Barton said "Later...maybe. Now, you only need to stop him from killing you."

"I will."

"Have compassion at the point of your ice axe," Greg went on. "And drive it to the center of him."

"I agree that it needs to be done," said Oliver.

CHAPTER NINETEEN

It was interesting to be in the pass, where they moved slowly through the middle, cautioned by large boulders. The walking was easy, done mostly on firm, snow-covered ground. It was guessed that warmer times of the year brought snow and rock from above, and that this was often a windy place. Not only was the snow deeper along the edges of the pass, but it was drifted to either side of the boulders, although predominantly toward the east.

Oliver moved them through to the crestline, and encountered the deeper snow of what promised to be a gradual descent to Gyubanare Glacier.

They stood before the scene.

"You'll walk eight hundred feet, before descending a couple hundred," said Oliver. "But I think it becomes steep near the glacier...and rockier."

Beyond the glacier was another mountain line which, straight across from them, showed similar altitude. It then ran north to at least twenty-one thousand feet, ending where the glacier went above it, westward, beneath the Nepal-Tibet face.

Molly asked "That's the one the group was wanting to climb? It would take a week, Oliver. I don't want to. Do you?"

He said "I think three days. But it was mainly for Norm. And although Bush seemed to want to, I think he'd be happy to climb any mountain close to twenty thousand feet. Maybe he doesn't need to do that." He looked at his watch. "I guess what the three of us do, depends on what happens when I meet Curt. It's now a bit after two. Do you want to rest before you go?"

Greg Barton took off his pack and placed it beside a boulder, which he sat on. Then he leaned back and looked toward the scene ahead. He muttered "Was it the green one?"

"What did you say?" Oliver raised his voice.

Greg looked at the ground, then ahead, ostensibly to view the mountains across the way. "I was day-dreaming. So…you want us to descend here. To go straight down. I don't have a good map, Oliver."

After he helped Molly with her pack, he got out his map and handed it to Greg.

Molly said "We're essentially through the pass, aren't we? We can see all around."

"I've used this chart before," said Greg. "This the German one. Schneider? From the fifties." But he only glanced at it.

"Just descend to the glacier," said Oliver. "And move south along the edge of it, if possible…far as you can before dark. Then…tomorrow morning look back. If I'm alive you'll see me. Otherwise, go down to this pass." He pointed at the map. "Head back to Lobuche, and contact the military. Tell them what happened."

"You're scaring me, Oliver!" said Molly.

He sat beside her and hugged her.

Greg Barton said "No! It was the blue one."

Oliver shouted "I'll boil water. Have something to eat! Greg…?"

"What?"

He was surprised at Greg's quick response.

"On the chart," said Oliver, "It's fifty four hundred meters down there…when you get to Gyubanare. That's lower than where we slept last night. I want you to go straight down. Molly…you take him down!"

Molly had tears in her eyes.

"Yeh…I know," said Greg. "But it's a different one."

Oliver got out his stove and told Molly to get it going. "There's a breeze coming up," he said. "You might need to set a tent and put the stove inside. Nah! Not enough time for that."

He unwrapped a candy bar and brought it to Greg, who looked up at him, without expression, and took it.

Oliver watched him eat some of it.

"It could be something else," said Greg. "Curt might have a gun."

Molly had the stove in beside a boulder and was trying to get it lit.

As Oliver stood up, intending to help her, Greg Barton said "It's easy! You are neat and clean, and travel Royal Nepal Executive Class. They put a red sticker on your bag…and say "Go right through, Sir!" Meaning, we don't check the privileged. That's how!"

"A gun! Why wouldn't he have used it, before now?" said Oliver.

Greg rocked back and forth several times before anwering. "Why is he so steady in his advance? Why is the bastard so sure?"

Molly warmed her hands, holding them inside her parka, but there was a flame in the stove, and she was watching it. Also, she was shivering.

A wind was coming up. He had noted minutes earlier that it was debatable whether or not the sky was yet blue. A haze had arrived rapidly, not with apparent depth or darkness, but with power to promise obscurity. He said "I have to change my thinking!" And though he figured neither of them could hear, he added "But what should I do?"

He looked at his watch, and made a decision.

Molly was staring at a covered pan on the stove.

"Get food from your pack, Molly! And your cup."

She brought it out from inside her parka. As she showed it to him she glanced up, making steady eye Contact, then reached to the end of her pack in order to get food.

After she was eating a candy bar, he got one from his pocket and had a bite from it. And, now that the water was hot, he filled her cup and his own, and had a drink.

"Molly...the situation has changed. We're going back through the pass. All three of us. When we get to the other side, I'll escort you two part way down the same trail we came up."

"Yes, let's do that, Oliver. Do you think Curt has made it out of the valley? But...whatever...I want to go with you!"

He poured water into a cup for Greg, and told Molly to melt more snow.

Molly said "Greg has found his wife."

"But when I talk with him he's very alert. I think he'll be all right…if we get him down."

She said "If he wants to go. Maybe he thinks he's all right now. Maybe…he is."

"Are you suggesting he stay?"

"No. Just that maybe it isn't altitude sickness that got him to see his wife."

"But we have to assume it is. We'll walk quickly through the pass…and then get him down. If I used my head better I would have done it sooner. When we stood on the other side, why didn't I think of it?"

"All three of us wanted to come this way, Oliver. And Greg's condition wasn't so scary, then. You know…I got really scared a few minutes ago. I wanted you to direct me entirely."

He brought a cup of water to Greg.

"It's understandable," said Greg. "She wants to be part of what happens to you…rather than be on Gyubanare Glacier tomorrow morning and be told about your death… by the emptiness."

Oliver said "Do you agree about all of us going back?"

"Sure I do! Why would I choose to desert you? Why would she?"

"But you've got to go immediately down the other side."

"What if I don't want to?"

"If I believe you're impaired due to altitude, I'll make you descend."

Greg Barton got up. He breathed deeply, and moved his arms through the air, as though to warm his muscles. Then he sighed. "That's fair, Oliver…if you promise to be fair."

Oliver said "When we arrive at the east edge...if you're not impaired, but I ask you to take Molly down, will you?"

"I don't know! I didn't hear you promise."

"I won't make you descend...unless you clearly show impairment...or ask you to take Molly down, unless death or injury seems certain if she stays."

Oliver looked away. "I want to be alone...a minute. While I'm gone, please have water...both of you."

He walked about a hundred feet toward the south wall, to where he had only snow and waist-high boulders near him.

Looking upward, he spoke.

"Sure!...there's a storm coming. In it...will my emotions be true to what is best? After my anger rages in the wind, can it be gone with it? And does adversity have this sadness, for the doing of what's right?"

"Oliver, if you hear the music calling...it'll be different from what Curt hears!"

His body jerked upward...then he turned to face Molly.

"Don't be embarrassed!" she said. "Is it so terrible to be discovered?"

"Molly...I don't think of God as a bearded old man. But...I do feel an awareness." He shrugged his shoulders. "There seems to be something beyond us. A presence. I believe sentience resides in all things. Think of the way an atom and things smaller than that, maintain themselves. And this is part of a consciousness." Again he shrugged. "We have "I"...and it seems we share it with an "I" which centers all existence."

"I pray every day, Oliver...to my personal God."

"Then you have a clear, simple truth," he said. "You have a bottom line, Molly...a unified field theory in your heart. As for me, I'm seeking mine, but it's the same as yours."

She said "I interrupted you. Please continue!"

She put the palm of her mitt to her face, and looked down, as though meaning to disappear.

"Molly, the only other thing I might do is quietly pay respect to my ancestors."

"Good idea! Go ahead!"

He looked at the side of the hill, then at her. "What about you" Don't you think you should honor yours?"

Looking upward, she said "Thanks!" She pointed at herself. "I hope you're happy you helped do this!"

Oliver hugged her. He then looked up and said "We'll do our best!"

Molly pushed her face against his chest, and whispered "They might be unimpressed by that."

He said "Probably it's our intentions they care about. Our hearts."

She said "Do you think they're here?"

"I hope so! We can use some help."

"Oliver, sometimes thoughts come to me as though someone else is talking. Is it from outside of me? Above? Or is it my inner voice?"

"Perhaps there's no difference, Molly. Do you hear any words now? I could use some advice."

"Sure I do, Oliver. I hear a crowd. This place was under the sea once...where life began."

"Molly...that's a key for you. It broadens your outlook."

"The single cells gathered, Oliver. Those inside needed blood to carry food and oxygen to them. Eyes came…and everything else. But…atoms formed the single cell, in the harmony of their movement…that awareness you speak of. And…smaller parts, yet, made the atoms. So…when does it stop? Can there be one thing?"

"To me…only consciousness can be one thing, in the sense of purpose, or needing other than itself to give any point to continuance."

"Do you mean love, Oliver?"

Oliver said "What are you and I, Molly…in our orbit? What do lovers do?"

"Yes…the answer is simple, isn't it?"

They kissed.

Greg Barton was waiting. He had put away Molly's stove and pan and cup, and leaned her pack against a boulder, and placed Oliver's beside it.

Oliver said "Sorry we took so much time. I think we were looking for a key."

"You found it, in my opinion."

"Greg, where will you go from Kathmandu?" Molly asked.

He didn't answer…but put on his pack.

Oliver tried to help. "Connecticut? You have two kids, there, by your first wife…you said."

"They're grown, and have families." Then he smiled, weakly. "Yes…I'll go there a couple weeks. And…to Kunming. This is here!"

"Is Kunming in China?" asked Molly.

Greg seemed to drift toward a question. He sighed, then cleared his throat. "Yes…it's in the southwest of China." He shrugged his shoulders. "It's a bit high in altitude, so it stays cool." He seemed to have become more alert. "If I went there, would you come to see me?"

Oliver said "Sure. Next October, maybe."

"But…" Molly began, "It depends on how many Faulkner's there are by that time."

CHAPTER TWENTY

Oliver was ahead of the others by a hundred feet, upon coming again to the eastern edge of Changri La.

He figured that the haze had originated in the southeast, it being dark and heavy that way. But the day was yet clear enough to see two tiny forms, one much larger than the other, at the base of the north-running part of Changri Nup. Perhaps Marlaine and Bush had been following the many tracks and now wondered about the single set departing up the middle.

Straight out, the glacier was a bit lower and appeared as two rounded humps of snow which seemed, even in the haze, very bright and white. And the valley of it continued up to an icewall a half mile away, to the northeast. So, it would be difficult to get out from between the humps, and if someone did that, and approached Changi La, they would be clearly visible.

Not far from him a basin occurred where the glacier touched the mountain line, at this pass, but it seemed to be not much of one, not deep…although, in the whiteness he wasn't certain.

He heard Molly. "There's no Curt?"

"I want to hold you!" Greg Barton said. "Come closer!"

Molly said "Who…come closer? Me?"

Greg jerked his thumb to his left. "No! Her!...that's Johanna!"

Molly got near Oliver, and whispered. "He was fine, all through the pass."

So Oliver didn't hesitate. Stepping to Greg, and putting a hand on his shoulder, he said "Mr. Barton. It could be that your wife is present. I'm not able to know the truth of that. But…often…cerebral edema can make you see what isn't there."

"I don't have that," Greg said, calmly.

"Maybe not. But you're seeing what you wanted to see early yesterday…and couldn't. I'm sending you down."

There was no answer. Greg looked at the ground straight ahead of himself, and to his left. Then in the same calm manner, said "My wife is here. Perhaps it's time for me to go with her."

"I have to send you down!" said Oliver. "And that's a fair decision. While you're in this life, you ought to honor its virtues and needs."

Greg Barton sighed, then again looked down. "My life is a concern of yours. Of course!"

Oliver now put his hand on Molly's shoulder, and spoke loudly, as he faced Greg. "The second part of my promise has to do with Molly. She's going with you. There's no other thing for me to do, if I love her."

Molly said "Why don't you say it to me?"

"There's no time for argument, Molly. Also, you've got to look after Mr. Barton." Again he faced Greg. "And you need to help her."

He put both arms around her and pulled her in, and when she resisted he wasn't surprised. But, as she looked up at him he guessed she already accepted it, and was merely sad.

There seemed to be no anger as they kissed.

"Now feel the storm outside, Oliver. You're right…I need to get Mr. Barton down. How far?"

"To where we slept last night. Then set up a tent for him… and us."

Greg Barton said, firmly, "Let's go, Molly!"

Oliver turned away and looked out over the glacier.

He tried to hear something of their departure, a footstep or voice, but heard nothing. He looked that way and saw Molly in the lead, her eyes on the ground. She saw him watching, and stopped. So, he waved, in order to say "I'll be seeing you!" but she perhaps misunderstood, and didn't wave back. Greg Barton did. Then they continued onward.

Oliver had put his walking stick against a boulder.

Now he took off his pack and leaned it there. He pushed his ice axe a couple inches into the firm snow, far enough for it to stand upright.

A distant shout came. Little words reached him, from Molly.

He waved, and whispered. "I love you, too."

And then they went around the bend.

Now it was thickly grey on the other side of the glacier, and appeared to be snowing there. And to the south it was quite dark, although the time was early, being just after four.

There was no sign of Curt on the glacier. Either he couldn't get out of it, or he would try farther north of the pass, in order to come back down to it. But Oliver was figuring what Curt would do if he had a map, and maybe he didn't.

Oliver walked several feet directly east, getting to the very edge of the pass, where he could view more of the glacier. But now, although he saw nothing unusual, he had a sudden feeling of danger. So he looked behind him, and all around.

Avalanche occurred…the hissing scrape of it seeming to come from just above. So he moved away, stepping sideways as he looked up. But there was nothing there.

A great cracking sound split the day. And then he knew the sound came from the middle of the pass.

He drove the shaft of his ice axe into the firm snow, and was expecting to meet the same texture under the crust, as a minute ago, but it went in easier and farther. Now digging with the axe and his boot he found a crust barely more than an inch thick, with powder under that. And his shaft went in about ten inches.

He had walked off the pass, and maybe that's why his senses warned him. Certainly this unsupported crust might break in a fight.

Before retreating, he decided to have a look with binoculars, and again scanned outward and a bit down. Then he saw a man's boot tracks. They were on the far side of the depression…and came in a straight line toward the pass.

Again he looked behind himself, and all around, but there was only snow and rock.

He retreated to where he left the pack and walking stick. Then he put his stiff mitts into the pack and got out his leather gloves. They were lined with sheepskin, but fit loosely and were well worn...so would be somewhat flexible, perhaps, even in the cold.

He wondered if Curt had seen him and was hiding in the depression.

Looking that way his eyes rested at the far side of it, where there was an overhang of snow. It was sculpted by the wind...and was smoothly done...was finely curved inward. And for awhile he saw it without thinking about it. Then he said "Molly, I feel it, too. It's not sand, it's snow...but there's a sameness, in accord with the wind."

That part of the snow was where Curt's head appeared, and where his form came slowly into full view. He was using his ice axe as a walking stick. He wore his hood up, and had goggles, and his moderately bearded face had much whiteness on it from gathered ice. And as he walked, he was looking at the ground, apparently unconcerned about being seen.

Now Curt stopped and, standing in a straighter way, removed his hood and raised his goggles. Taking off his right hand mitt, he unzipped his parka and reached inside, holding this pose for a full minute. Then he removed the other mitt, and slapped his hands together. He put on the mitts, lowered the goggles to his eyes, and walked onward.

Curt was swaggering. As he used his axe as a cane, he posed with it at the end of each rolling step. There was a hesitation followed by unnecessary contact between the axe's shaft point and the snow.

In this strutting, Oliver saw Curt saying he was the dominant man, and a confident one. But, Oliver wondered if Curt believed in his superiority…or was, perhaps, playing to an audience where he wanted two to believe it.

Oliver tried to be impersonal. There came a murderer, strutting.

Sure, he and Curt were the same, deep inside, where the soul is, where the light is. But…he, Oliver, needed to honor the sameness by knowing they were different, otherwise.

He only contended with Curt's acts on this side of Curt's wall…which began somewhere far away…and ended here.

Curt was now distant a hundred feet. He yet strutted, and acted fully superior and confident. And so he came in this manner to within fifty feet, where he stopped. Again he removed his hood and raised his goggles. Then, without evident emotion, he shouted "Why don't you run away?"

Oliver didn't answer.

But, he decided to enter Curt's world, a step. And it seemed that the man was at his wall, was in a place this side of the last time he loved. Why all the need to pose, otherwise? Why the need to strut if there were no fear of emptiness in that place?

Oliver said "Why would I run away?"

Curt held back his head and laughed. Then he shouted, "Because you know what's ahead. But your legs are shaky and weak and trembly…so you can't run. But you can beg! Do that! Get on your knees!"

Oliver held his ice axe chest-high. "I'm not trembling, Curt. You are."

Curt laughed again, but louder than before.

Oliver said, "You're crying in the dark...but the only part that knows it is the trembling part."

Curt bellowed. "What would I be afraid of?"

"I don't know! You're afraid at your wall...but I was never at it."

There was silence.

Curt removed the mitt from his right hand, and again reached inside his parka.

A distant shout entered. It was Molly. "He has a gun!"

Oliver didn't look at her, not wanting to draw attention that way. And neither did Curt look.

He said "Curt...that part of you which is here touching things...the world needs to be rid of."

Curt came to twenty feet away, and stopped. He said "I don't need a gun. I killed Hu Dhou of China, who was famous at the top...who was invincible on his wall." He laughed. "I'm bigger than you...and stronger, and quicker...and I have skills learned in the military and other top places...and I know from direct contact with slaughtered sheep. Ha, ha, ha. You're dead!"

"Why did you stop to tell me?" Oliver said.

Curt said "You didn't tell the army about Shoree. You wanted me to come here!" Curt shrugged his shoulders. "Ah!...you stand low in my ratings...inferior. You should run! And tell your wife to. If you don't, your ghost will watch me use her...as I did Shoree. Ha, ha, ha. Then I'll take your money and hers. I'll cut off your heads and roll them into the gulley I passed through."

"No!" said Oliver. "You won't be doing that!"

Curt said "Most of my opponents were smarter than you. They knew how to talk. Your friend in New Hampshire... Elmer?...said he could fire me, that he might terminate the contract. And so I put this into his back." He reached to an outside pocket, low on his parka, and withdrew the icepick knife. He waved it, and returned it. "Shall I use it?...or beat you to death? How do you want to die?"

Oliver could see no reason to answer.

Curt went on. "Elmer deserved the knife...sitting on his hill. And so does Oliver Faulkner...at the top. Ha, ha, ha."

Oliver said "I'm at the bottom. Those who know what is permanent...are at the top."

"I killed my father...when I was eight. And I might have killed my mother, too...if she didn't leave town."

Oliver said "Then...long before that...and just after this...is the best part."

Curt looked down at his ice axe which he held by his side, the point of it touching the snow. Now he rested it against a leg, as he closed his parka by using the zipper. But...the ax fell to the ground. As he bent to retrieve it, with his eyes on the tool, he suddenly jerked his head upward toward Oliver, as though he saw movement and was startled by it. He picked up the axe quickly and, holding it in both hands, took a deep breath.

Now Curt stepped forward, as though to deny his fear.

Oliver went to meet him.

Curt raised his axe, and bellowed. Then...with face muscles twisted...eyes opened wide, and having a wildness in them...he lunged ahead and brought down the axe toward Oliver.

Oliver turned his head to the right, and leaned backward...and he began to move his right leg, the one about to bear the weight of his shifting body. But his boot hit a rock.

The axe tore into the parka sleeve and hit his arm, a glancing blow. So...he was twisting his body as he fell. Then...as his right hand touched the ground, he was looking at Curt over his left shoulder.

Curt must have expected the axe to make solid contact. When it didn't he, too, lost his balance. But not by much. He stepped forward with his right leg, a few inches, and leaned his upper body downward.

Oliver...yet off balance...reached his left hand to Curt's right shoulder...and pulled toward himself...but only for an instant...then he let go and continued to the ground.

Curt was swinging his axe in a backhand motion toward Oliver's left leg.

He missed. And now they both were down.

Oliver, who had been facing the ground, leaped to his feet and, in the same effort...the same motion...raised his axe. Curt, who was looking up at him, tensed his muscles, as though getting ready to move.

Oliver drove in the point of his axe, hard as he could... so he wouldn't need to do it twice.

He stepped away from the body a short distance, toward the glacier, and stood looking at the ground. But, what he was seeing was Curt's head...as he hit it. Then...for mental ease...he stopped seeing that, and became aware, mostly, of the falling snow touching his face.

Molly arrived. And when he was hugging her, he saw Greg Barton in the snowy grayness...at the edge of things, walking away.

Molly held her face up to his, so he kissed her.

"Oliver...I thought he had a gun. Did you trip on a rock? I planned to jump on his back...but suddenly it was over. I was scared! Well...he's dead now. Oliver, look how dark it is...toward the other side of the glacier."

"Where is Greg Barton?" he asked.

"Gone. He left awhile ago. Said he would go down to where we had the tent last night. Then he hugged me and said he knew why I needed to be with you."

"He was just behind you, Molly."

They looked toward the south corner. Greg Barton was gone.

Now seeing Curt's body, he was struck by the appearance. It was face down, the head and shoulders low...the back and butt high. The left arm was extended to the rear, the hand of it palm up...and his right arm was hidden underneath. The ice axe was attached to his head, but all you could see of it was the end of the shaft, raised beyond his right shoulder.

Molly said "See how dark it is over there, in the storm. But why isn't it warmer, if it's coming from the south?"

"I think it came from the west," he said, "And struck below us. Where is your pack?"

"About three hundred feet down the trail. I can find it."

"Try to find mine, sweetheart...it's over there!" He pointed.

He went alone to Curt and removed the axe. Then he pushed the body onto its side, and straightened it. He put the goggles over the eyes and, after pulling up the hood, secured it at the neck. He reached for the parka zipper.

"He didn't have a gun?" Molly asked.

Kneeling, and looking inside the parka, he saw a pocket in the lining of it, and there was a wool shirt with pockets.

Molly kneeled. "Oliver...why was he putting his hand in there? Only to warm it?"

He felt in the shirt and found nothing. Then...from the pocket of the parka's lining he brought out a little plastic bag and held it in his hand. Near Molly.

"What's in it?" she said, putting her gloved hands around his.

He dumped the contents onto his hand.

"Oliver...it's two locks of hair."

He returned the hair to the bag, and put the bag back into the pocket...which had a zipper, so he closed it.

He asked Molly to help him drag the body to where he tested the snow, earlier...and ten minutes passed doing that, so the day got darker, and the snow was coming harder.

He hacked the crust with his axe, and kicked at it, making a place about ten inches deep. Then they dragged the body into it, and began covering it with snow.

"What are we honoring, Oliver? Not that I don't want to do this. I do! I'm glad he's dead...but...I agree to do this!"

He kicked more snow onto it.

"So...what...?" she said. "What's to mourn? Not that I think there is nothing."

"Molly...I believe every man is the same...at the center. Way inside...hidden...even the worst of men has that point of light. That's what I'm honoring. Otherwise, I feel like crap."

"Because you had to kill a man?"

"Yeh...we can talk about it, later."

Molly said "When I think of those he murdered...it hurts. But this doesn't...except...I feel sad...at what?"

He looked down at the body. "The murderousness is dead. What's to mourn here? There's a shape in the snow."

"Oliver...I think you're right to honor it."

He scraped and kicked more snow onto the body, and tamped it down. Then he laid Curt's ice axe on top of it.

"Molly, now we'll honor Shoree...and Norm...and the little boy, Curt could have saved."

She leaned hard against him, and said "Is it time to go? I'm cold, Oliver. The storm is here."

A gust of wind hit them.

He put his arms around her, and said "Kiss me, Molly, and I'll take you home."

And so...they kissed.

CHAPTER TWENTY ONE

In the deep-gray snowiness they departed Changri La and, after moving around the bend, slowly went down to where Molly left her pack...finding it because a handkerchief was tied on, and fluttering in the wind. Greg Barton must have done it.

Then they descended in darkness, and were hit by several powerful gusts.

At the previous night's camp, Greg Barton wasn't there, and neither was his tent. As they put their shelter alee of a boulder, they were sad to think of their friend wandering in the storm. Then, remembering that when Greg departed Changri La, it was snowing but not yet storming...they were happy to think he descended a half hour through the moderate snowfall...and the gray day...at least to the promontory, and probably much farther.

In the morning it was sunny, but late, when they got down to the glacier. Bush and Marlaine were there, and said they didn't see Greg Barton, but saw his tent down the trail. Oliver spoke about his fight with Curt. Then Bush and Marlaine began climbing toward Changri La, and he and Molly watched awhile.

They went to Gorak Shep, and on to Lobuche. But, the people in both places said they didn't see Greg Barton.

The sergeant and the Sherpa lady were gone, and he and Molly spent a quiet evening in the same little place.

The following day, late in the afternoon, Bush and Marlaine came in. They said they got to Changri La, and walked through to the other side...and saw Greg Barton sitting on a rock. He was dead. Of course, when walking to him they didn't think he was dead; his back was to them, and his hood was up. He seemed to be merely looking out across the glacier, on a sunny, blue-sky day.

They got his passport and wallet without disturbing him...and left him that way.

Bush said that after returning to this side of Changri La, they saw the ice axe...and where Curt was buried. There was a shape in the snow.

Made in the USA
Middletown, DE
01 December 2023